Tim Francis lives in Bristol and is a renowned screenwriter and media producer.
He is passionate about creating non formulaic, unconventional stories that excite his audience.
Previously he was Britain's most successful male model which brought him to the world of commercial and independent filmmaking.
He is now also a renewable energy expert specialising in solar.

To Roger

All the very best

Tim

WHAT IS A SCREEN NOVEL?

To be honest, I'm not sure… it just panned out that way.

My first dabble into writing was a tortuous episode in my teens, back in the Sixties of applying as little pressure as physically possible on my portable manual Olympia typewriter, so as not to thump through the ceiling of my council house bedroom floor and irritate my dad – even more so than playing Jimi Hendrix and The Who on my record player or not considering a job opportunity at Avonmouth Docks instead of going to university. At the time, my brother was an office equipment salesman and for some reason, the only paper he could purloin for me to type on was very thin and bright yellow - I think it was the copy paper used by secretaries and I'm sure it might've kick-started a bout of migraines which persisted into my 30's?

Anyway, I cobbled together several comedy sketches and was tutored through the post via The Royal Mail by The TV Scriptwriters School GB & America based in the Isle of Wight. Brian Blessed and Colin Welland would mark my canary-coloured papers (remember Chariots of Fire and 'The Brits are coming..' speech?) and they were always encouraging and kind and I'm sure were somehow instrumental in Benny Hill and the Two Ronnies using some of my one-liners. So, this experience - my first foray into unknown media territory was enough for me to realise that whatever background you came from and whatever talent one had, could one day be revisited for whatever fate lay ahead. It would be several decades on into the mid-Eighties during my modelling 'career' and working with commercial/film directors looking for film scripts, that I picked up the baton/pen and started writing again - *screenplays*.

Screenplays were a totally different discipline to master compared to sketches and stories I had written, based around the traditional book/novels I was familiar with. By the mid Nineties I had secured five writing commissions, four options and had a low budget film produced that I had co-written, 'Steps' starring Ron Moody. Screenplays were exactly that; a play written for the screen, whereby every scene was a text of visual imagery, whereas a well-written novel induced the reader to interpret their own imagined theatre.

I have often given up on many novels, finding the story structure too long and too immersed in superfluous background criteria or chapters that were fillers and did not progress the narrative but only showcased how much research the author had invested. With **a screen novel** my attempt – and it is no more than that – is to create a reality of each scene on the page so that the reader's journey is in real time with the characters, as opposed to portraying a retrospective account of incidents, so that the readers' experiences are shared with the story's cast as the tale unfolds.

So, as a professed 'hi-fi' buff audiophile I'm asking you to go 'vinyl' and not 'stream', to detox from your programmed book-reading habits – i.e. your 'encoding' and get 'decoded', so that you can enter a new zone of absorbed reading...a journey where the travelling holds centre stage with its destination - I truly hope you enjoy the ride.

The Dude Scribe Abides with and for you.

Tim Francis

Published in the UK by Clueless CIC

First Published 2021
www.cluelesspublishing.co.uk
Copyright © 2020 Tim Francis & Clueless CIC.
All rights reserved.

ISBN No. 978-1-8383112-0-9
A copy of this book has been deposited
and recorded at the British Library.

Success is not the position where you stand,
but the direction in which you look.

Acknowledgements

⚙ Thank you to my wife, Caroline for her rigour, patience, support and belief in me on a long hard road and to my daughters Rachel and Olivia for their love and faith.

⚙ To James Taylor, the fashion photographer who first told me about Welsh Gold during a modelling photo-shoot back in the mid-eighties.

⚙ To Wayne Thomas of the historic Tower Colliery, in the Cynon Valley of South Wales, the oldest working deep coal mine in the UK and possibly the world, until its closure in 2008. A true Welsh coal miner who took me to the coal face, where I met other miners who would later tell me the legendary story of a clutch of miners in the Sixties who bought their mine against all odds and retired to Spain…having stumbled upon the Mother Lode… Aur Cymru - Welsh Gold.

⚙ To those who either commissioned, inspired or championed my 'scribe corner' and put precious time aside to read and often advise on my ramblings: David Jones, Jonathan Tammuz, Tim Crowden, Brian Leith, Laurie Lee, Dianne Dreyer, Kelly le Brock, Jean Diamond, Simon Beaufoy, Minta Townshend, Alan Sutton, Jeremy Fraser, Jemma Wadham, Kim Hicks, Joyce Hissey, Anton Mullan, Annie Bates, Paul McGann, Rod Steiger, Gene Simmons (Kiss), Nigel Havers, Brian Blessed, Colin Welland, Vadim Jean, Liam Cunningham, Toyah Wilcox, Paul Henry, Billy Prince, Ed Baney, Steve Hodges, Mike Francis and Benny Hill and The Two Ronnies who bought a teenager's comedy sketches back in the day…

⚙ And finally to my close friend Matt Bagg, a true 'Prospector' in life, whose vision, integrity and entrepreneurial flair for a new approach in the 'business' of life, was the lead instrument in orchestrating 'The Great British Gold Rush' and taking it to market

EDITED BY: Corrina Mackenzie, Anthony Bagg & Simon Fraser.
PRINTED BY: eazyprint.co.uk

Deep Harmony

Sweet is the work, my God, my king,
To praise Thy name, give thanks and sing,
To show Thy love by morning light
And talk of all Thy truth at night.

Sweet is the day of sacred rest,
No mortal cares shall seize my breast.
O may my heart in tune be found,
Like David's harp of solemn sound!

Then shall I see, and hear, and know
All I desired and wished below;
And every power find sweet employ
In that eternal world of joy.

Since the Nationalisation of British coal in 1947, over 8000 miners had been killed.
By 1969, at least 17,000 more had died from lung disease.
The only occupation more hazardous than coal mining was war itself.

Some were
luckier than others...

Big Hewett responds, 'And if you do, you weren't there.'

Pennant switches off from the banter and senses something,

'Quiet!' The crew are still in party mode, Pennant loses his patience, 'QUIET!'

The crew stop cavorting and listen. Davy's all ears,

'I don't hear anything man?'

Wallace's cough irritates the silence. Pennant strains harder to locate the noise, tunes in to the ether...

The belief in the existence of supernatural creatures and strange sounds like the 'Knocker' or 'Bwca' in Welsh (which was a miniature grizzled dwarf who would hammer on pit-props to cause a cave-in) was a way for miners to deal with strange events and accidents.

Pennant tries to rise above such ingrained portent,

'Nor me. I felt it.'

Big Hewett bumps his head on the ceiling. Pennant gently feels around an overhead outcrop, brushes coal dust away, revealing rock.

'Sedimentary...galena, sandstone...quartz...this is one screwed up seam we're working.'

Big Hewett comments, 'Drills 'll testify to that.'

Davy quanders the exhibit, 'Reckon the rock's moved?'

All look up. The ceiling sheds grit into Wallace's eyes. The atmosphere flips like a coin. Pennant tilts his head to filter the whining breeze, shouts,

'Grab a prop all of you, now!'

Pennant rams his prop midway under the large rock embedded in the roof. The earth shifts, a corrugated roof sheet buckles, showers Pennant's eyes with rubble. He's blind and choking. A support arm snaps. They scramble to underpin the cross strut. Pennant shoves Davy,

'Out!' Suddenly the massive boulder drops. The ground shakes. Dust clears, revealing the crew encircling the giant stone 'bell'.

Back on the roadway, the crew follow a clattering coal-extraction conveyor belt. Pennant's heroism has sapped him, he looks wearily ahead, he stoops and rests his hands on his knees, pretending all's well. Davy rubs his aching knee, takes out some wacky-baccy to chew. Pennant comments,

'Show's over for G30 lads, it's slim pickings now.'

'You okay?' Davy offers to help Pennant up but gets the cold shoulder,

'Upset your karma did it?' then less brittle,

'You lot go on, get cleaned up, cocktails and coal dust don't mix.'

Big Hewett tries to keep the conversation more agreeable,

'That was some boulder, what d'you reckon it weighed? The tenor bell at Llandrillo Parish was five hundredweight, made a beautiful sound it did.'

Pennant sombrely comments, 'For whom the bell tolls eh?'

Big Hewett replies, 'But that was bigger, fill it with solid rock and that mother's got to be four or five tons at least.'

Pennant's patience is wearing thin, 'We almost got milled back there and you're prattling on playing guess-the-weight?' Pennant sits down, breathing heavily,

'I just need a minute.'

Davy hovers near Pennant, 'No worries man, we'll hang on - - '

'Wanna watch me take a shit too d'you?' He produces

a newspaper,

'I've got an arse wipe.'

Davy lingers, knows Pennant's spent but proud. Davy concedes, 'Okay boys.' Davy and the crew move on.

Pennant's guilt niggles concerning his hostility to his crew, he calls out but they're out of ear-shot,

'Forgive me boys...call me a party pooper.'

Later. Pennant's light-bulb flickers – he taps his helmet-lamp. A gale-force air-current peppers his white eye-band with coal-dust, thrown up from their boots downwind. Exhausted, as their lights grow distant, his eyes begin to close.

****

Back at the colliery changing rooms, racks of weather-beaten work clothes hang as the crew shower. Taffy's soapy hand reaches for his shampoo bottle, realises that the NUM leader, 'Pit-Bull Grady' (Rocker) and his colossal brother, The Eclipse, have nicked it. Everybody's learnt to give these two psycho-arseholes wide berth. Davy's about to say something but Taffy stops him and whispers, 'That'd be a 'bald' move,' as he shows Davy a bottle of Immac Hair Remover he's refilled the shampoo bottle with. They watch Grady, mystified at the lack of lather, as he massages his scalp, tapping and cursing the antiquated showers. Davy and Taffy leak a smile.

****

Standing behind the counter to the Lamp Room, an Attendant looks up from a safety mining lamp he's checking and sighs as he clocks the veteran, Old Man Avery, approach. The old man starts studying a rack of numbered metal identity tags, one hook especially that only has a triangular tally and not a return shift round brass tag. It swings slowly in the draft and settles in his hand.
The Attendant's resigned to this routine,
'You still 'ere?' Old Man Avery doesn't look up,
'You're a man short.'
'Listen pop, yesterday, today, tomorrow 'll be just the same, you can't come in. You know that.'
Avery turns and faces him,
'Two hundred and forty-three I make it from the morning shift.'
The Attendant reaches and takes the brass tag, returns it to the board hook, stating,
'Look, some gappers forget to hand 'em in.' Avery's not buying it and responds,

'Floating colliers I've allowed for.'

The Attendant ponders the observation,

'Know what I reckon? I reckon you've earned y'self a lie in after all these years, don't you? He clicks the lamp switch, the light flickers.

****

Beneath the lamp room, a mile back to the Roadway, Pennant's helmet torch glimmers and dies. He wakes, still woozy, stands and sways, adjusting his squint at the sign above the coal-extraction conveyor belt, *'MAN-RIDING STRICTLY FORBIDDEN'*. Tempted to hop on the belt, he thinks better of it, resigned to the long walk ahead until he notices something glint on the passing belt amongst the coal.

He clambers onto the belt. The canvas tongue pitches over bullet-hard rollers, like gritted black teeth chattering. His prostrate body adjusts, finds refuge amongst the vibrating coal. His helmet feels oppressive, so he removes it, rubs his bald head. Overhead lights pass by at intervals. An out-crop of granite skims his cranium by microns, draws blood. Sod that. He replaces his helmet. Again, his lamp flickers but it's enough to catch a glimpse of something shining on the belt ahead, then, somewhere, amongst the agitated black lumps, it's gone. Perplexed, he props himself up on his elbow to find it.

Up ahead, a mile downwind, a timber roof support creaks, bulges outwards and splits, dislodging a thin, corrugated metal roof sheet which hangs diagonally into the shadows – a switchblade released like the sound of a curtain being drawn.

A Shillydigone beetle-moth, scuttles out of the splintered beam onto the metal guillotine, remains still.

On the approaching rattling belt, its passenger kneels, starts to crawl, reaches forward, intrigue now obsessive, as Pennant discards one lump after another. Something registers in his veteran gaze. He reaches forward, s-t-r-e-t-c-h-ing to his limit. He seizes it! Smiling and contented, he flashes the gold incisor.

Up ahead the corrugated sheet hangs...

Suddenly, the jutting metal sheet looms, severing his head from his shoulders! Pennant's empty hand twitches.

POSSESSED

In the terraced street of Pitman's Row, almost dead centre, stood number 79. Built from industrial red brick, possibly the hardest brick ever baked, these 19th century miners' cottages with their roofs made from local slate, were built to endure the elements.

One element in particular, not weather related I'll admit, but naturally formed by nature, with the atomic number 79, is the dense, lustrous precious metal *GOLD*. As this was Davy's cottage and as the free-spirited hippy was totally unaware of the significance of the mellow yellow numbers above his door knocker, which he had passed by every day since birth, some might call it a tad ironic.

Inside the cottage, a beaten-up alarm clock rings on a bedside table, its raucous sound bleeds into the small bedroom like a piercing warning bell. Davy kills the sound, switches on a bedside lava lamp – in its glow, a guitar rests against a psychedelic

John Lennon wall poster, above a wooden dresser. It's propping up a stack of LPs with the outer album cover: *Cream - Wheels of Fire*. Directly above, *Pink Floyd's Ummagumma* album sits on top of a Ferguson record player. Propped behind it stands the record sleeve to *Jimi Hendrix - Axis Bold As Love*.

Davy's lean torso harbours blued bruises and scars, part evident under a white, cotton, string vest. His whole counterculture identity seems at odds with the 'guest room's' pink floral-gold wallpaper and matching lampshade. On the carpet sits every true hippy's marijuana smoking must-have, a mandatory ornate brass shisha pipe. Next to this lie several books, *'On the Road' by Jack Kerouac*, *'Stranger in a Strange Land' by Robert Heinlein* and *Irwin Shaw's, 'Rich Man, Poor Man'*. He rubs his swollen knee, finds only one chewed sandal and glares at the toy poodle, who just snuck in, guarding the other soggy, gnawed sandal.

The door flings open. Davy's sister, Peggy, pops her blond bouffant head around the door and informs him,

'There's been an accident at the mine.'

Outside, dawn's promise yawns its way into the Vale of Merthyr, as mist spills down into the isolated coal-mining community. In the Colliery Yard, fence-to-fence miners hold strike placards demanding safety improvements. An air of dissension hangs. A Union Official hands out propaganda leaflets.

A suited Coal Board Manager, Tarrant, 40s, arrives in a Jag', parks near the Colliery Main Office. He gets out, rich smooth attire, cold manner, eyes that miss nothing. He checks a blemish on the car paintwork. Somebody hands him a leaflet. Bevan, late 40s, a Production Supervisor, emerges from the office and greets him. Tarrant studies the gathering as Bevan brings him up to speed,

'Third fatality this month.' Tarrant looks up beyond the gathering and focuses on a winch wheel.

'Know him well?' Tarrant asks.

'We all did. Pennant's old school, best Face Captain there was', Bevan replies.

'How'd it happen?'

'Seems...he fell asleep...on the belt.' Tarrant turns, faces Bevan, 'What the hell possessed the man to - - '

'It's out of character, Pennant's regarded as something of a hero 'round here,' Bevan informs him.

'That's all we bloody need.'

Davy and his crew thread their way to the front of the assembly. Tarrant squeezes the leaflet to a ball and follows Bevan into the office.

A Secretary, Valma, late 20s, Celtic features of undecided beauty, appears from the annex room with a tea-tray and hands Tarrant a tea mug. Something in Tarrant's salacious manner makes her self-conscious, 'Later love.'

He brushes past her and goes outside. Bevan and Valma watch him face the music. Davy catches Valma's eye.

Tarrant boxes clever, the raucous crowd hear him out as he speaks,

'My dad was a Yorkshire miner, he had a saying, 'The first forty years are the 'ardest' and this big wheel's had its lion's share of 'em. But wheels are no good if they're not turning. Now I sympathise with your grievances, at a time when the Coal

Board's looking for mines to close. But as long as that wheel isn't turning, you'll go to the top of the list.'

Davy responds, 'We don't need your sympathy, we need - - '

Tarrant cuts him dead, 'To go home and rest up! Enjoy your well-earned weekend. Then ask your wives and kids where they think their next meal's coming from?' He lets that sink in.

'So, see you all here, <u>all</u> of you, Monday.'

****

A cluster of customers gather at Llewellyn's fish shop in the village to watch a replay of the *'Apollo 11 lunar landing'* on a wall-mounted monochrome TV.

On the counter, a newspaper heading with a photo of the moon: *'WHAT WILL THEY DISCOVER?'* as cockles and mussels squirm and settle on the front page's 'moon's surface'. Mr Llewellyn, 50's, wraps the contents for an obese elderly lady, Mrs Hughes, who pays and greets all with a bubbly *'Hello'* as she jiggle-squeezes past Lyn (Taffy's missus) and Peggy (Davy's sister). Peggy's in a Mary Quant inspired PVC mac with white high-heels and make-up OD to match (if Dusty Springfield had a twin sister!) – she is glued to the BBC London TV broadcast.

Outside, two teenage girls blast pop music from a transistor radio, *Thunderclap Newman's 'Something In the Air'*. Peggy's sigh translates as 'Fat chance' as she comments,

'London...might as well be the bleedin' moon.'

A young mother, Susan, 20's, enters with a pram. Peggy's poodle, Dusty, can smell the baby, sniffs around. Llewellyn, the shop owner, greets Peggy,

'Ow do Miss Johnson?' As Peggy pulls out four pink tupperware containers and plonks them on the counter.

'Just had them in.' Peggy says, as Lyn pops a lid to one of the very pink containers,

'Glad you're keepin' yourself busy pet, that's good.' Lyn says, as Llewellyn looks underwhelmed at the demo and asks,

'Just the pink is it?' Peggy stacks them, the job lot has been dispatched,

'It's what you ordered.' To which Lyn adds her tuppence-worth,

'That's right, I saw you tick the bloody form meself.'

Llewellyn concedes, knows better than to argue with these two and scoops up the pink pile. Lyn turns to Peggy,

'How's y' brother? My Taffy's a bit down.'

'Shook 'im it did, Pennant's been...well, a sort of guardian angel to them,' Peggy responds.

'S'pose he is now.' Lyn reflects matter-of-factly.

'Me brother feels guilty for 'aving left 'im.'

'Well he shouldn't. Taffy heard Pennant tell your Davy to bugger off, he was old enough to know better.' Lyn's disrespectful tirade hangs in the shop's silence, so she quickly changes the subject,

'Heard you're trying to sell y' mum's place? If there's anything I can do pet?' Peggy exhales,

'Not really, still sortin' all the stuff...she was worse than dad, found 'er old war ration coupons.' Both take in the tired decor, just as it was then maybe? Lyn's head gestures toward Llewellyn, 'E might still take 'em.' Their cackling wakes up the baby which starts crying. Lyn mouths a soft 'Sorry' to Sue and aside to Peggy, adding,

'Didn't ration that though did they?' Hoots of laughter as Mrs Reece, 40's, enters, met by stony, hostile silence – like somebody flicked the fun button to 'off'. Llewellyn rises above the politics, smiles at Mrs Reece,

'Be with you in a minute luv'. 'Ow's your 'usband?' Lyn responds acidically in Welsh,

'Ti'n syrfo gwragedd bradwrs fynhun y't' *(Serve scab's wives here do you?)* Llewellyn replies with a stern smile, 'Age old strikes don't concern me...we've all a right to eat.' Lyn's out for blood,

'Really? Say that to the all the miner's widows 'ere do you?' Lyn turns to leave, the Young Mother with pram, about-turns to join her. Peggy's hovering. Llewellyn referees in exasperation, 'Here you lot! What about this haddock?!'

Lyn yanks the shop door open, the bell rings – final round, she turns,

'Got a bleedin' cat 'aven't you?! Come on Peg.' The gaggle of women exit.

IT'S GOING TO BE SUNNY

Ma Hewett was the village oracle and over the years, her terraced cottage lounge had become a mini theatre for her soothsaying performances. And on July 20th 1969, the night-time moon seemed to glow a little brighter as Davy, crew, and the proud, loyal women-folk gathered.

On a table, two goldfish, one black, one gold, glide and glint under a lamp shade, the bowl reflecting an indoor rainbow. Behind the table, a huge crack runs vertically up the wall like a lightning zap bolt. Big Hewett shows Davy a Coal Board disclaimer letter,

'Bloody Swiss cheese we're living above.' Hewett says, Davy responds,

'Yeh man, try selling me mum's place. How old d' they reckon these coals seams are?' Big Hewett squeezes the letter,

'Won't say 'cos if they ain't theirs they can't know and if they don't know - - ' Davy concludes,

'They ain't liable. Bastards. Come the revolution man.' An air of anticipation fills the room as Peggy watches Ma Hewett invert a tea-cup onto a saucer, and asks,

'What's it to be Mrs Hewett?' Taffy sits forward and asks,

'Should we strike?' Ma Hewett stares at the tea-leaf pattern, eyes narrow, as she announces,

'I see...a stone...you're touching it...connected to money - - ' Peggy looks at Davy,

'Could be our ma's headstone?' Ma Hewett mulls that and responds,

'Perhaps...but no...beyond the grave...deeper...' Davy dwells on his conscience,

'Or Pennant's...crazy diamond, it should never have happened.' Big Hewett puts his hand on Davy's shoulder,

'There's no blame with us Davy, any of us, so don't beat yourself up.' Taffy endorses that thought,

'Sure thing boyo, just couldn't figure it me'self, with his experience.' Ma Hewett journeys on through her trance-state,

'I'm seeing the colours black...or...' Peggy watches the goldfish intertwine in a slow ballet, fascinated but suspenseful, she asks,

'Or what Mrs Hewett?' Ma Hewett looks up and says,

'AUR...gold luv.' Everyone's bemused. Davy looks cynical... doesn't realise that, for some reason, his eyes are transfixed on the goldfish bowl, a microcosmic metaphor presaging something his wacky-baccy might help to tap into... But right now, Ma Hewett's sounding like a sea-side fortune teller, he tests her,

'What d'you reckon 'bout this Prince Charlie then?' Ma Hewett looks down, something about the leaves. 'Can't be trusted...not with them ears.' Peggy nudges Davy to ask about the mine, Davy obliges,

'What about the mine Mrs Hewett? What's gonna happen about the strike 'n all?'

After a long pause, Ma Hewett lifts her head up...the answer's coming...

'A voice...from above, will tell you...' Taffy's missus, Lyn asks,

'Tell 'em what love?' Ma Hewett responds like it's unquestionable,

'To strike - - ' Taffy's incredulous,

'Strike?!'

Ma continues, ' - - while the iron's hot. You must go back...down.'

Davy looks at the crew, 'Looks like we're going back lads.'

Ma Hewett fixes Davy with an imploring gaze,

'You, Davy, must lead your boys.' Davy shifts uncomfortably,

'Whoa there ma, they're not my boys, I mean I'm not lead material - - '

Ma's not having any of it, 'You Davy! You must seize the dragon's tail!'

Davy jokes dismissively, looks at Big Hewett,

'Sure those are just tea leaves your Ma's drinking? Ma Hewett speaks slowly, an intense proclamation in Welsh,

'Fe glywi di lais oddi fry...yn dy arwain' *(You'll hear a voice from above...it will guide you)*.

She looks out of the window, beyond the net curtains into the dark night,

'It's going to be Sunny.' Exhausted she collapses into Davy's arms, he laughs awkwardly.

'Who said I wasn't working?' Avery squints like he's in denial. Davy probes further,

'What? Counting miners clocking in and going home?'

'Some don't go home. It's all about numbers you see.' Avery replies.

'But not being able to join them?' Davy says.

'Wouldn't want to do that, be a liability, at my age.' Davy's surprised at that revelation and says,

'But everybody here thinks...'

'They do? No, one last look would do me, see what's changed. Mines are living organisms you see.'

The old man turns away, wipes his eyes with a handkerchief and resumes his watch, clutching the whistle.

Distant hills and valleys stretch beyond the horizon. Davy feels like some audition's over. He stubs out his joint and leaves the old boy to it. After a few steps, he looks back at the sad figure, feels guilty somehow. Old Man Avery faces the coal-pit, says nothing, drinks in the landscape.

PAPER, STONE AND SCISSORS

Beyond the colliery building which houses the main office, the miners changing rooms, lockers and store room, lies the *Winding House* gantry. Across the main courtyard miners climb a metal grid stairwell and arrive at the mine's pit-head entrance, where three red signs hang over the cage grill: *'NO SMOKING' 'NO CONTRABAND'* and to the side, *'MAXIMUM LOAD .9 TONNES'.* Davy joins Taffy and Big Hewett, who is carrying his canary. Against a wall to one side, on the approach to the elevator cage, stands the operator behind a battered wooden counter. The cage operator officially known as the Banksman, takes one of a duplicate brass identity tag from a check-board, the last of 12 in a section, hooked amongst rows of others, marked *'FACE CAPTAIN - JOHNSON',* Davy reacts,

'Hey, that's not mine.'

'Tis now.' The Banksman looks at Davy, who turns to his crew saying,

'Come on boys, with my knee? No way man, anyway I'm not the oldest.' Taffy flips his eye-patch,

'And I'd need both to keep an eye on you two.' Big Hewett massages his unsteady, numb black-nailed hands and holds them up,

'Not with these boys, wouldn't want t' place y' fate in these hands.' Taffy asserts himself,

'Look, we're professionals, right? So let's act like...them. What we need's a hi-level management decision.' The crew look corporate for just a nano-beat then launch into to paper-stone-scissors. Several rat-tat-tat bouts. Davy tries hard to lose but keeps winning,

'Shit man!' Big Hewett shares his wisdom,

'See...it's in the leaves.' Davy's concedes,

'Do me a favour man, next time buy y' ma a jar of coffee.'

The early morning shift finds Davy and his crew shoulder-to-shoulder in a cage with eight other miners. The metal basket squeals and vibrates as it descends into darkness, countered by their helmet lights clicking on in unison. Big Hewett's beam scans Taffy's outfit – the tux and bow-tie, nobody blinks, like it's normal attire down here. The cage jams to a halt, then falls – a shriek of tortured steel for 30 feet until the cables yank it to a dead stop. It creakily coasts, resuming normal pace. Nobody's bothered, just alert. Davy eases the tension, mimics a department store lift with latin musak played on tools/kit. Taffy joins in.

At the bottom of the pit head the cage crunks to ground level, the grill shunts open. Joke over. A bell rings. The atmosphere's charged with urgency as miners gather. Shafts of light bob through the assembly towards them. Two soaked miners jostle past with their water-sodden, groaning casualty on a stretcher - a young Jamaican miner, early 20s, whose bloodied limp arm hangs down, several fingers missing, as they enter the cage. Behind them Bevan, Production Super and rocker Deputy, Pit-Bull Grady, step forward. Bevan shouts,

'FOR CHRIST'S SAKE SOMEBODY KILL THAT SODDIN - - ' The bell stops, instant hush. Except for a whistling breeze. Bevan checks his pocket-watch, then the gathering,

'Thank-you. Right boys, you may 'ave gathered, there's been another accident, not fatal, thank God, but one like last Friday's that could 'ave been avoided! Read the bloody signs!'

Davy removes his helmet. One by one, the rest follow, paying homage. Bevan's goaded in to an ad hoc ritual,

'Okay, let's 'ave a minute's for Pennant.' Blanket silence. Time ticks. A pit-prop creaks, then another, closer, spikes the stillness. Each time, wrings nerves a little tighter, spooking Sunny the pit pony who whinnies and stumbles into his handler. Davy looks over. Bevan replaces his helmet. One-by-one, others follow. Davy comments aside to his crew,

'Funny how the minutes get shorter and the hours longer.' Bevan re-asserts his authority,

'A reminder. Anyone caught hopping on the band 'll be 'opping out of 'ere even faster!' One miner responds,

'Maybe 'e was too shagged out like most of us 'ere working these shifts?!' Another miner adjusts his helmet,

'Ow do we know it wasn't a fall-in?!' A 3rd miner,

'Or explosion?!' A 4th miner shouts.

'BLACK DAMP!' General rumblings build. Bevan holds up a methanometer,

'ALRIGHT, THAT'S ENOUGH! According to this it's safe to breathe.' Miners move off to their respective seams, past a notice, *'National Coal Board Mines & Quarries Act 1954. TIMBER...'* Bevan's not done yet,

'Read the notice! Local timber's expensive, that's why we're importing these.' He grabs a PIT-PROP as Big Hewett prises a beetle from his neck. It draws blood,

'And these buggers - - ' He flings it down and stamps on it. Davy nods to Bevan,

'Be coal next.' Bevan picks up a corrugated metal roof sheet,

'They're as safe as timber if you shore 'em up properly! Right! We get paid for digging coal not chatting!'

Davy, crew and miners move off to their respective seams.

Sunny the pit pony won't budge. The Handler tries a pinch of snuff. Sunny's head jolts back in a sneezing spasm. Davy gives the animal a comforting pat as Bevan remembers a small detail,

'Oh, I forgot to mention – bit of a sensitive subject at this time I know, but...I may as well come out with it – could you all keep a look-out for a head?'

'EVER SMELT VIOLETS?'

The roadway is the link route to various coal seams, wide enough to drive a car through and wide enough for Bevan, Grady, and a young lad in tow, to walk three abreast. Hot on Davy's heels, the youngest of the trio being Dino Ferrera, late teens, Italian, a cocky mod in stylish work-wear. Bevan calls out to Davy and his crew ahead,

'Just a moment boys. Who's in charge now?' The crew point to Davy.

'Right you are. Davy, meet...'

Davy's pace slows, but he's still walking. Bevan nudges the lad to speak up.

'You've a tongue lad.' Dino responds,

'Dino...Ferrera.' Davy stops walking, turns.

'Ferrera?' Grady enlightens him,

'Old man owns the trattoria.' Davy faces the lad,

'What you doing here Die?' The lad replies,

'It's Dino.'

'If you think your old man's kitchen was hot.' Dino keeps pace as they walk. Bevan adds,

'E's 'ad a few weeks up top.' Davy senses the favour coming, stops, turns to face them, as Taffy comments,

'Really. Find any coal?' Grady sneers at Taffy's tuxedo, pops some chewing tobacco and spits at his feet,

'Still dressing in the dark?' Bevan gets it back on track,

'You're a man short. Two, if Wallace don't show. So management's decided some young blood 'll be - - ' Davy interjects,

'On my hands? No way, bad scene man. Look, I didn't want this gig.'

Grady goads Davy, 'Iti or blackie, we've got 'em both for starters, your choice brother?'

Davy responds, 'Who'd tell the difference down here man?'

'Just show 'im the ropes.' Bevan implores.

'Enough to hang himself? There's other crews.' Davy insists.

'They're full.' Bevan informs him.

'What about the stretcher case? That'll need a - - '

'Got a gapper there now.'

'Shit. There's no free lunches here man.' Davy stares at Bevan and Grady.

'Or is there? Look, we're pushing ahead on a new seam.' Davy informs him.

'Then another hand would be - - ' Bevan interrupts.

'It's too dangerous man!' Davy protests as he holds up his lamp to Dino like a trial exhibit.

'Alright Die' (thinks real hard) 'If there's no blue in my flame or it's fading man, what does that tell you?'

Like a hung jury, Bevan, Grady, and Davy wait for the answer, Dino responds,

'We all gonna die?' Bevan nods, 'Good answer.' Grady contributes, 'You betcha your I-ti arse.'

Davy studies Dino's padded outfit.

'He's clean? Right?' Grady and Bevan look uneasy. Grady searches the kid like a border patrol, finds cigarettes and a radio. Bevan spells it out to the kid,

'Can't you read? No watches, no radios, no cigarettes.' Dino cuts him off,

'No shit.'

'Setting up shop are we Die?' Davy comments. Bevan's not smiling. Looks at the lad, sighs and leaves.

Dino straightens his collar. Grady gobs tobacco spittle on Dino's boot, grabs the contraband and transistor radio from him.

'Bad reception down 'ere boy.' Davy walks, Dino scoots after him. Grady's hostile gaze watches the duo leave.

'What's 'ees problem?' Dino asks Davy.

'Ees problem? Man.' Davy shakes his head, exasperated.

Further along the roadway, Davy and Dino pass through a thick metal air-lock door. As they emerge on the other side – *PHWAA!* A wind-rush hits them. A Hauler pulls a nearby wall-cable that runs along the roadway, sounding a bell. A red light flashes as coal trollies rumble by on rails. Dino looks like he just entered the forbidden planet, stares down the endless tunnel into infinity. Rubs the toe of his new Doc' Martin boots.

'I hope those are comfortable Die?' Dino clocks Davy's sandals, suppresses a smirk. Another torrent of air buffets them, throwing up a dust-swirl.

'Sheesh!' Dino looks vexed. Davy enlightens him, shouts above the pressure wave,

'That's the ventometer. It just blew you a kiss.'

'A kiss?'

'The biggest fan you've got down here. Ever smelt violets? They're flowers man.'

'It's gonna give me flowers too?'

'It's no joke man, there's a certain fragrance.'

'Ah, viola...ci...kindova...sweet smelling?'

'Ci...and deadly man. 'Cos if you smell 'em and that breaks down, we all gonna die.'

Further along the roadway, Taffy and Big Hewett round a bend, find a tall stack of pit props, like the sample Bevan had.

Taffy reaches up and lifts the top beam, releasing a hoard of beetles that hail down into their clothing. Both freak. Taffy and Big Hewett start stripping, frantically unbuttoning shirts, trousers – the full monty – and commence a frenzied dance, stark naked, slapping themselves and stamping on beetles in a crazy rhythm.

Approaching them, half a mile downwind, Dino follows Davy as they pass several spent seams and weathered signs: *'POPPY FIELDS'*, *'DIEPPE'*, *'ARRAS'* and *'DR40'*. Dino sneaks a peek past the DR40 sign. The Eclipse, with a mining crew, spots him.

'Hey, sandals, watch y' boy!' Dino saunters back toward Davy, who reads the situation calmly.

'Stay on the roadway Die', you dig?' The Eclipse strides over,

'Unless 'e's planning on wearing the roof as a hat?' Davy stands between the Eclipse and Dino,

'He's cool man.'

'Cool?! Y' best put y' bitch on a lead.' Dino's jaw tightens. The Eclipse grabs Davy by his pig-tail.

'Hey man! Watch the hairnet!' Dino walks up to The Eclipse, says nothing, just stares.

'I think y' mutt needs some discipline. Sit boy.' Dino kicks him in the groin. The Eclipse's massive bulk folds, groaning as Dino knees him in the head. The Crew and Davy are stunned. This kid's one hard-arse mod. Dino follows Davy, who breaks into a reluctant stride.

'You alright Meester Johnson?' Davy, wide-eyed, manages a nod, straightens his hairnet as they beat a retreat.

Around a turning in the roadway, they lose sight of the Eclipse and crew. Davy's still shaking his head. Dino's not bothered, it's a stroll in the park.

'Look man, I'm a pacifist and I've got to work with these crews! You've been down 'ere less than an hour an' you're strutting around like a dog with two dicks.'

'Non sono un cane Meester Johnson, he is dog who needs lesson.'

'Lessons?! I'm the teacher here, OK? You might as well have cut my dick off! I can fight my own battles!'

'I thought a pacifist doesn't fight Meester Johnson?'

'I mean...stop calling me Meester Johnson! Jesus! I'm supposed to be your boss, someone you look up to.' Dino's blank expression at Davy's torn hair-net draped over one ear. Davy tucks it back, resumes walking.

Davy, the reluctant Face Captain, spells out what's required.

'The more you dig the more bread you make, goes with the territory – like the risks.' Dino bristles excitedly.

'That gets you off? Shit, throw a lump of coal down here and you'll hit a dozen war heroes man. Wanna prove something? Prove you can use these.' Davy tugs his ear lobe.

Dino taps his ear like a headset, 'Coming through loud and clear Meester Johnson.'

'Good. 'Cos if you don't hear it, see it or smell it, doesn't mean it isn't there.'

'What ees not there?'

'Better tap 'em again kid. *Danger*. Like most women, it has its bad periods and like most men, you'll wonder what hit you.' Dino ponders that, looks amused,

'You talk as if the mine were a - - ' Davy interjects,

'Yeah, welcome to Gaia's womb. Ever read Greek mythology man? Think of her as your Earth Mother, the Goddess of Uranus, 'cos down here, your arse is hers, so show her some respect and expect a few scratches from this bella donna.'

As they walk, Dino turns to Davy,

Y'know the Greek hippy stuff back there about Gaia 'n all? Ees good you even thought I'd understand eet shows respect. I mean, my old man never tell me anything, he just beat the crap out of me when he wasn't bitching about how I's screwing things up, 'thees plate's chipped', 'there's a dirty fork'.'

'And what's he think about you being down here?'

'Whoa! No disrespect but he thinks mining's the worst job in...in Gaia man! The pits!'

Davy laughs.

'Out of the frying pan yeah?'

'That's about it, down here, I'm a gonna burn in Hell as far as papa's concerned.'

'Wheels of fire man.' Davy stops walking, fixes Dino with an earnest eye.

'Down here, nobody's gonna burn 'cos nobody's gonna screw up. You dig?'

'I plan to Meester Johnson.'

A little later, Dino stops, his boots hurt but he won't let on. Davy resumes his lesson plan on foot.

'Look, down here, don't be too proud to take advice, especially from my crew, they're skilled technicians.'

He looks at Dino's boots.

'Might save you a lot of pain in the long run.'

'So, you can tell your old man that mining's changed, you can tell him...about the highly skilled technicians you work with, about the high standards of safety and stringent codes of practice, some you won't understand at first, so don't be too proud to ask.'

As they turn a corner, Taffy and Big Hewett are naked, checking each other's orifices for beetles. Dino looks at Davy, words forming...Davy answers,

'Don't ask.'

THREE SIXES

Outside his terraced cottage, just a stone's throw from the mine, Old Man Avery begins his daily routine, he checks his pocket watch, looks ahead at the pit head gantry as he sets off. He looks up again, a ritual to check if the winch wheel is turning...slowly with controlled revolutions, and almost collides with 'Toby Jug' Wallace, who's late for his shift. Wallace seems troubled by a black Labrador dog following him, he glances back, coughing, almost retching as he shivers.

'Bloody thing, won't stop following me.' He erupts in a coughing seizure, stamps his foot at the dog,

'Go on – shoo! Off 'ome!'

Avery informs him, 'That's what he's trying to do – that's Pennant's dog. Lucky.'

'I thought black dogs were s'posed to be unlucky?' Avery notices Wallace's shoe lace is undone,

'Mind y' don't trip on that.'

Wallace looks ill, shaking as he ties it. It breaks, lands looped like a '6'. Avery looks at Wallace's house number, '66'. Though unspoken, a miner's superstition is tested. Avery places his hand on Wallace's shoulder.

'There's always tomorrow's shift. You need to get yourself to bed.'

Wallace shrugs off Avery's empathetic hand.

'Some of us 'ave to work.'

****

On route to the new seam, the crew carrying timber props fork left in to tunnel, where they arrive at, what looks like, a deep wide cavern in the ground with little room to manoeuvre. Taffy and Big Hewett take the lead, edge past, overtly dramatic, passing timbers along whilst pressing hard against the rock face. They look back at Dino to follow. The kid with some trepidation follows suit, looks back at Davy...who steps in to the hole and walks on the water's surface?! The still shallow pond's mirror reflection of the shaft above shatters as Davy splashes through the pond. Taffy aside to Dino,

'He'll be baptising you next Die.'

two tweets.

Back on the Roadway, a Pit Overman, Jonesy shouts to Davy and his crew above the wind-rush.

'Heard a tremor – everything alright?!' Then he gets a whiff of Big Hewett.

'Jeezuz, what's that? New beetle repellant?' Big Hewett's not amused, Jonesy addresses the crew,

'Been lookin' for you lot, there's water building on G30!' Davy replies,

'How bad?!'

'Knees in under five I reckon, before it reaches you lot!' Looks at Big Hewett and Dino,

'Good news for the turd twins eh? Couple pumps should do it!' Davy turns to his crew,

'Right! You go on.' Big Hewett asks,

'What about y' star pupil?' Indicating Dino. Davy with a resigned sigh gives Dino a nod to help him.

****

At the Pit-head, above the vertical coal shaft, eleven miners and Morgan, a Pit-Overman, board the elevator cage. The grill shuts as the air-lock door opposite opens. Wallace's rotund form dashes through, waving his tommy-box.

'Old it, stop! Wait boys!'

The descent is abruptly interrupted as the lever's wrenched back to stop. Miners judder to a halt. *Know that sound new leather makes? Well this is steel cables stretching...not such a pleasing sound now is it?* One miner comments,

'Toby Jug forgot 'is lunch.' Another miner eyeballs Wallace,

'Always one slow arse-wipe, forget y' balls if they weren't in a bag.' Morgan's superstition kicks in but he masks it, abiding to regulations,

'Thirteen's one too many lads.' As he's about to pull the lever somebody shouts,

'What if you leave y' wallet up top?' That should do it!' Sniggers abound. Morgan's getting an ulcer. He erupts.

'Them's the rules!' Silence. Taut steel cables whisper to the suspended cage. Wallace presses his pale, quivering face against the grill, imploring blood-shot eyes like rivets.

'Look lads, for Christ sakes, none get paid 'til we're at the face! So please...stop y' buggerin' about!' Morgan concedes.

'Alright! Open the bloody hatch.' The safety grill is yanked open followed by the hatch gate. Wallace boards and shoe-horns himself inside. The grill slams shut, then the hatch gate. Morgan grips the lever, hesitates, swallows and pulls the lever.

Outside, silhouetted against dawn's mist the winch-wheel turns... slowly at first, then the revolutions start to gather momentum... becoming faster and faster, underscored by a cacophony of creaking steel and distant cries.

THE DRAGON'S TAIL

Early evening at the local District Post War Memorial Hospital, Davy, with head-plaster, sits upright in a ward bed, in a partly curtained off bay. Peggy, Big Hewett, and Taffy are leaving as a Doctor checks his chart and exits. Davy manages a weak wave as they leave, then settles back into his pillow to rest. His eyelids start to close, but, in a semi-slumber, he senses someone standing at the foot of the bed. Old Man Avery appears, gags, looks pale, startles Davy. He removes his cap and places it in the canvas bag he's holding in his limp arm.

'You alright son?' The old man enquires, as he pulls a chair near and sits.

The hippy miner's not in the mood for entertaining the geriatric, but peace and love get the better.

'Whaat? Oh...yeah, just the usual.' Rubs his knee as Avery coughs again. 'Should be asking you that.'

'How's the boy?' Davy props himself up more...this could be

a long sit in.

'Trying to rest, they've got him under observation.'

'Hurt himself did 'e?'

'Had a seizure.' This seems more than casual interest for the old man.

'What sort of seizure?' Now the pleasant conversations turning into an enquiry.

'Hey man, I don't know, I'm no doctor – it was a fit of some sort, lack of oxygen they reckon.'

'*Epilepsy.* My brother was a sufferer. Is the kid prone to them?'

'*I don't know*...Jesus, it was my first day as...' Struggles to say it' ...and his first day...*mining*' Ironic snort.

'M'brother always got a warning with them, he'd see a...kind of aura he'd call it.' The old man tells him but Davy's only tuned in to his own trauma.

'First day man! With a year's worth of shit thrown in for good measure. Lucky they found us when they did.' Davy relives the moment, finds it difficult to swallow.

Avery pours him a glass of water from a bedside table jug. Davy takes a sip, looks at the light from an overhead lamp, refracting in the glass. Davy ponders the vision. Did he dream it? Looks up and notices Avery's observing him, as if he's sharing his dream-scape. Or maybe the old boy's here 'cos he's lonely? That's more like it, get real man. Awkward silence. Avery stands up, puts the chair back where he found it and turns to Davy.

'Did they say how long they're keeping you in?'

'Few days they reckon.' He taps his knee. 'Sort this out if they can.'

a psychiatrist's couch.

'Well, that was after I'd seen...this tail, like a serpent's...glowing as it...swept through the water.'

'Like a Welsh Dragon perhaps?' This is nuts. Davy snaps out of sharing Avery's madness.

'This is crazy man, all of it, and don't forget the medication that... Doctor Kildare's got me on.'

Avery reaches into his canvas holdall and pulls out something heavy, size of a crow-bar wrapped in gold chenille.

'What's next pop? Let me guess...a clarinet? You're gonna do an Acker Bilk number...'Stranger on the Shore'?'

'No, even though they took that song to the moon...didn't know that did you? No, this is more mother earth bound...more fitting because this mother won't give up her little treasure easily. That's why you're going to need this.'

The mysterious object thunks onto the bed.

'Well...aren't you going to unwrap it?'

Davy unfolds the gold fabric to reveal a blackened steel drill bit. Davy, the engineer, picks it up and seems transfixed by the weight and wavy patterns, like dark blades of grass murmuring in the wind he can almost hear. Avery enlightens him.

'Hypnotic aren't they? The swirls – like the sands of time locked in steel – watered steel to be precise, banded carbide forged with vanadium. Same technique they used with sword making a thousand years ago in the Middle East. Damascus steel, hardest there is, keeps its edge you see, became somewhat of a legend during the Crusades, quite appropriate really.' Davy looks up.

'Crusades? Gee pop...where d'you get this? I mean, this is dark art, off the charts man, not exactly standard coal board issue.'

'It's not exactly coal that's the issue here. A Syrian blacksmith forged it for me many years ago, never got the chance to use it, until now. You'll need it to fight this Welsh dragon.' Davy recalls Ma Hewett's prophecy, *'You must seize the dragon's tail!'* Is someone trying to tell Davy something?

The old boy puts his cap on, seems contented. Coughs, recovers, to prise a smile and starts shuffling out. Davy hurriedly wraps the drill-bit and calls out.

'Wait! Hold on a minute pop, you've got the wrong dude. I'm no gold prospector, I'm – I'm a coal miner!'

Avery stops and turns.

'I know. And those prospects seem pretty bleak now don't they?'

'This isn't Virginia or the Yukon man,' Davy states.

'Ah, just as well, they call them sourdoughs there, doesn't have the same ring as being a prospector, does it?'

'But this is Wales man,' proclaims Davy.

'Even better, Welsh gold's the rarest there is.' Avery takes a step and points at the drill-bit,

'When that can't cut it, you best visit a friend of mine...Tibsy... best speak up when you do, virtually deaf now from working with explosives...that's what they did, still do, with the Jamaicans, put 'em in the front line...how he lost his arm.'

Davy tries to process his thought response but only manages to choke on his food,

'Whoa there! Tibsy? A one-armed black dude handling explosives?'

'He had my old place...after my brother passed on he was a sort of brother too, in a way...when you're down there.' The Old Man looks down, dwells on that thought for a moment, then raises his head,

'Retired now...he'd need a hand setting the charges these days, but he can advise you...otherwise, he's usually spot on.'

Davy's eyes widen as he visualises the scene whilst gazing at his hands...his treasured metacarpus intactus!

'Usually?!

Avery's about to leave but does a half turn,

'You know...the Ancient Roman's knew, got a taste of it in Dolaucothi and Pumsaint, Carmarthen, but...I think they were too far north...where as you...may have just hit the jackpot. See you tomorrow.'

Davy watches the old boy slowly exit, his coughs becoming distant. He studies the swirls in the Damascus steel, blinks to fight its hypnotic quality, his eyes start to close.

Outside the hospital Avery finds Lucky, the black Labrador, waiting. He pats the dog, a tryst with destiny. As Lucky tries to follow him home, Avery bends down and strokes the dog,

'Best get you home to Pennant's place, she'll be needing some company.'

****

Inside the hospital ward Davy heads for the toilet on a crutch. He rests the crutch against the door frame and enters. Seated on the loo in a dressing gown, he checks the door lock as he smokes a joint. The pain in his knee eases as he drifts away.

Across the corridor, in a small lounge area, two elderly ladies in night robes are recuperating watching a BBC broadcast on a black and white TV: the Prince of Wales' Investiture. Madge, an octogenarian with a blue rinse perm, comments on the spectacle. 'Be nice if he met a local girl.'

Back in the loo, Davy's tripping. Sunny the Pit-Pony is talking to him, using the sink as a water trough. Davy searches his pyjamas.

'Oh Jesus, what did I do with that - - '

Sunny peers over his blinkers.

'Nugget?' Sunny winnies, laughs, cranking up Davy's frustration.

'Hey man, if this is real, then they'll have to believe me, with or without the Old Man's...' searches for the word, Sunny helps him.

'Nugget?' He winnies again. Davy's exasperation manifests as a stutter as he takes another hit from his spliff.

'It's – it's – not about size man - - ' Sunny responds.

'Sure it isn't...it's the thought that counts...only, without it, you might as well be talkin' moon-rocks.'

Davy's conviction wrestles with his drowsy euphoria.

'Even the Romans missed it man, they screwed up, went too far north!'

'The Romans screwed up?' Sunny asks.

'Yeah man, it's – it's about the Syrian sword thing too man, the crusades and that Mother Lode he's been searching for, for...700 years was it?'

'Try Miles...I think he said miles.'

'Right! 700 man! Down the line, north to south, every mine mapped and logged and dug...*Doug*'! His dead brother was there man, I mean alive at the time...a geologist who knows Mother Earth rocks! Hey, d'you get it?! *It rocks man!* And his brother, Old Man Avery was a cartographer man!

I mean that's like the perfect duet man, that's Simon and Garfunkel, without guitars (sings) *'I am a rock, I am an island'.* Can you dig that? All those years, mapping, logging, digging, searching...then more mapping, digging and'...gets confused 'more logging...?' Sunny yawns, adding

'I get the picture.'

'All those years...him and his brother...and this black dude Tibsy.' Sunny counts on his hoof,

'I make that three.'

Davy's still in Doug remembrance mode,

'Rest in peace brother.' A reverent beat broken by Sunny.

'So, I take it you're sold on all this Welsh Gold shit?'

'Hey man, I didn't say that, what I'm saying is - - ' Outside somebody bangs the door. Davy looks back at Sunny, now sporting a headband of dazzling gold, crunching from a bag labelled '22 CARATS' who comments,

'When opportunity knocks?'

Davy emerges from the bathroom on his crutch, shuffles past Madge with a double-take reality check at her pantone perm, mutters to himself, *'Now I'm seeing blue hair?'*

'Hey, I could 'ear you chatting, is somebody still in there?' Davy glances across at the lounge TV and sees *'Mr Ed'* the U.S. talking horse sitcom which weirds him out even more, validating his Dr Doolittle drug-induced abilities.

'A little hoarse.' He pats his chest and then Madge's perm. 'Must be the drugs.'

BEER'S OFF

Early evening outside the local Public House, metallic hinges creak as wind whips *'The Griffin'* sign. Inside, by the tarnished wooden bar, stands Taffy, above him a row of tankards and a toby jug hang. The Landlord respectfully removes Wallace's toby jug, Taffy looks uneasy but the Landlord places it in a cardboard box clinking as it joins a posthumous collection.

'Getting heavier by the day.' He closes the lid and places it gently under the bar.

'Getting to be a shrine.' He reaches for another inscribed *'Taffy Cleeves'* which swings and settles as he grabs it. In the background lounge small sombre clusters of regulars sit, some couples but mainly miners of all ages staring at their beer glasses, conversing in low tones. The Landlady, Vera, nicotine-thin, mid-fifties in a mauve paisley pattern nylon dress does the rounds, collecting empty glasses.

'Closing early tonight lads.' Gloomy nods all around. The Landlord asks Taffy, 'Usual Taff'?' Taffy, seldom lost for words, nods. The beer pump sputters an egg cup's worth of dregs into Taffy's tankard.

Grady and his gargantuan brother, The Eclipse, sporting Dino's head bruise, arrive, start handing out union strike leaflets. Big Hewett enters. The Landlady returns, puts a towel over the pump and looks at Grady and his brother, thinking, *are they losing their hair?* She calls out,

'Beer's off fellas, sorry. I can do bottles but it's extra.' Big Hewett nods to Taffy and the Landlady. She places two bottles on the bar and stares at Grady who also nods at her.

'Ere? What you done to y' hair?' The Eclipse has his back to her. The Landlady shrieks.

'And im! Who's been cuttin' it? Where's y' lovely Elvis quiff?' Taffy looks uncomfortable, asks the Landlady,

'How much do I owe you Vera?' She takes Taffy's fiver. The brothers are not enjoying this line of enquiry. Still fathoming the brother's depilation, she gives Taffy his change and calls out. 'What shampoo you two using?' Taffy grabs the unopened bottles – about to slink away but Grady blocks his path.

'Can't drink those. Top's still on.' Grady takes one and opens it with his teeth. He puts the opened bottle down, psyches Taffy with a '*your turn*' glare. The Landlady intervenes,

'Ere, don't be silly boys, let me - - ', but Grady puts his hand up to prevent her.

Taffy stiffens, tries it. A dull crunch emits from his mouth. He puts the second bottle down, successfully opened and smiles, displaying the new gap in his lower front teeth, as he spits the broken incisor tooth out. Big Hewett steps forward as support for Taffy, as the Eclipse grabs the last bottle and nestles it between his buttocks...slowly smiles and *pphtt*, pops the top and places the third open bottle on the bar. Grady gives a 'sport' commentary.

'M'brother does it wiv 'eads too – best tell that to y' pot head boss and his Iti' bitch, 'cos next time he won't make hospital.'

An air of tension hangs. The Landlady notices another 'deceased' tankard, takes it down and starts placing it in the box, adding.

'Being laid off's one thing, laid to rest's another. Show a bit of respect lads.'

The Eclipse fixes his gaze on Big Hewett and mumbles,

'Got you down for number 9 scrum half against Trelewis Colliery'

Big Hewett's perplexed expression doesn't seem to change for a few frozen seconds,

'Number 9?! I haven't touched a rugby ball since school.'

Grady intervenes,

'Then big fella, you best get some practice in before the weekend, hadn't you?' Grady draws closer. 'You wouldn't wanna let y'brothers down now would you?'

An air of tension hangs. Big Hewett shakes his head as Taffy comments with a thoughtful suggestion,

'I've got some baggy safari shorts you can have.'

The brothers grab their beer bottles, eye the gathering with disdain as Grady spits on the floorboards as they exit.

Moments later a young career couple enter, hesitate in the doorway but clock Vera's welcoming smile.

'Come on in pet, we don't bite.'

The career girl, early 20's, struts to the bar with her suited 'arm candy' boyfriend, orders a dry Martini, lights a cigarette, flaunts the gold watch. Taffy and Big Hewett return to their table and observe the couple – alien anachronisms. The Landlord's Wife, Vera, relishes the change from the usual riffraff. Glasses clink, laughter now almost seems disrespectful. Big Hewett comments. 'That's the future that is,' Taffy replies.

'And it's not from round 'ere.' Big Hewett begins to hum the Welsh ballad, *Deep Harmony*. One by one, Taffy and others join him. Gradually, the rest of the pub unites, singing in harmony the valedictory hymn. The volume builds, drowning the bar's party chatter.

****

Next day, at the Pit Gates, protesting miners are on strike, a larger group than before, led by Grady and The Eclipse, who collide with police protecting defiant workers. From the side-lines, womenfolk scream abuse at the police and the scabs. Two police officers grapple with The Eclipse as his fist pistons into a seasoned black miner in the second row, battling to get to his shift.

****

Sunday morning at the local church, Davy, his Crew, Bevan, Tarrant, and Valma, amidst scores of other miners and family members, gather to attend the mass funeral service. Valma looks across from the opposite pew and allows herself a formal smile at Davy. The local parish vicar steps up into the pulpit to address the congregation as one of the miner's widows starts weeping.

Davy adjusts his ill-fitting dark suit jacket that belonged to his dad, feels uneasy with the sartorial convention. A welcome distraction grabs his attention as his eyes fix on a gold crucifix above the altar, which he knows is not real but its divine lustre seems to compel him in a sotto voce to say, *'It's not real'.* Big Hewett misinterprets and consoles Davy, whispering,

'I know Davy, hard to believe.'

After the service, as people leave the cemetery, Davy visits his father's grave in another plot. It starts to rain as a gust of wind rustles the branches of a nearby tree. He pulls his collar up and retrieves a bandana from his pocket, securing his hair as he brushes leaves from the headstone, *'REGINALD ISAAC JOHNSON, 1901-1964, FACE-CAPTAIN, PERISHED IN THE MINING DISASTER.'* In his pocket handkerchief, Davy carefully unwraps the filling-sized gold nugget. He steps closer to touch the grave headstone, but grimaces as his knee begins to throb.

He lights up a spliff, inhales deeply...notices a white rabbit that hops behind the gravestone and seems to disappear? Davy begins to stare through the grave...hearing Ma Hewett's prescient voice, *'Connected to money...beyond the grave... deeper...'* and in the perceived dark stillness below, Davy sees a dragon's tail of gold dust shimmer in a pool of water, awakened from its slumber by rain droplets falling from the ceiling above.

****

Inside the Colliery Social Club, a night-time meeting ensues. In the large hall, a sea of seated Miners sit cradling their plastic cups of beer. Irreverent fury spasmodically erupts from the attendees. On a raised stage, several Officials, and Bevan, sit behind a rostrum where Tarrant stands. Loud bellows ring out – it's a free for all.

'...safety regulations which clearly state - - '

Davy and crew arrive, near the back entrance, collect a cup of beer from a side table. The Eclipse clocks Dino, bristles, but Grady lobs him a 'not here' glare. Several miners take offence at the lecture, stand and rant at Tarrant as he continues.

' - - which clearly state a cage load not to exceed twelve persons - - ' A mining Spokesman speaks out,

'And why risk it, we ask?! 'Cos until we're half mile under and a mile out sloggin' our balls off, none get paid!'

Davy looks down at his cup of beer and sees a snake-ridge of foam floating above the glinting amber liquid. Tarrant draws the proceedings to a close.

'You wanna show of hands?! Well, so do I! On the bloody job! You've got two days to get back to work. You strike, WE SHUT SHOP!'

Tarrant and his officials exit the hall, jeers ring out as Dino arrives. Bevan remains, pacifying what has become an unruly mob.

'ALRIGHT!! You've heard Mr Tarrant's proposal,' Bevan says. Heated discussions as Miners take ballot forms.

'So, are we going to shut up or shut down?!' a Spokesman calls out.

'Vote wisely! The board 'as promised to review current conditions - - ,' Bevan says but is interrupted as Grady jumps on the stage platform and tears his ballot paper into pieces, shouting,

'Don't need no ballot, a show of hands 'll do! Who's with me?!'

Uneasy mumblings as the miners stop heading towards the ballot box. Bevan shakes his head and reminds them,

'That's not the norm.'

'But thirteen dead miners is?!' Grady replies. 'Anybody 'ave a problem with that?!' Grady scours the gathering, looks threateningly towards Davy and his crew. Nobody says a word. Grady raises his hand...the Spokesman's next, others follow. A blaze of hands joined by Taffy and Big Hewett but Davy's not so sure. Dino likewise, smiles at Davy. It's unanimous. Grady looks at Bevan, as if to say *'there's your answer'*. Bevan says in a sorrowful tone,

'Now it's the mine's funeral.' Bevan says as he lowers his head in disbelief and exits.

'Motion carried!' Proclaims Grady.

WHITE RABBIT

Late evening, outside the Colliery Social Club, scores of miners head back home. Davy is joined by Dino, who runs to catch up with him.

'You should've voted,' Davy says.

'Why?' Dino replies.

'Why make enemies?' Davy asks.

'You deedn't raise your hand either,' Dino says.

'I've got my reasons,' replies Davy.

'And your crew have theirs?' Dino responds. Davy loses his rag, the kid's becoming a bit cocky.

'Some's got dependants man! They were digging coal when you were digging sandpits!' Davy calms down. 'Look, if the mine's mothballed...it could be for good...then we may never know.'

'Know what?' Dino asks. Davy takes out a joint and lights it, inhales, becomes pensive.

'Look kid, I appreciate your support man, sticking up for me when you...but it won't change anything.'

'Change what Meester Johnson? I don't get you?' Dino's question seems laced with desperation that he may lose his job. Davy sympathises, takes another long hit from his joint and breaks the news gently,

'It's for your own good man...mining...it's just not your bag man, it's a bad fit...shit man, I didn't mean it that way but...medically speaking you'd be a danger to yourself and the crew.' Davy doesn't notice Dino sneer and continues the discourse,

'I know that it all seems heroic as a young dude, battling against the elements, mods versus rockers – but there's more casualties than heroes man.' Davy's eyes burn and fill.

'You think Taffy's eye patch is fancy dress? That Hew can't hold a drink 'cos he's a wanker?!' He eases his bad knee, rubs it and continues his speech,

'Oh, they joke about it man but that's pride man. If they had their chance again - - '

Dino laughs, which stops Davy walking, he turns, confused and tetchy, facing Dino.

'Did I say something funny man?' Davy asks, unaware that he's offended the kid.

'You theenk I wanna go back down there with you and your crew?' Dino's pride and arrogance hits Davy like a stun-bullet.

'What's that man?' says Davy.

'You theenk some romantica notion got me down there? It was a laugh, sometheeng a leetle different, beet hairy. Heroic? Tstch. All I saw was a bunch of tired old - - '

Davy throws a punch, which somehow goes wide of the mark.

Dino's response jab is quicker, connects with Davy's jaw, he folds like a puppet's strings just got snipped. Dino's vitriol mellows, he bends to help Davy to his feet but the crumpled hippy pulls away, rubbing his jaw, and stumbles awkwardly, jolting his bad knee.

'Sorry Meester Johnson, it was just a reflex, I thought you were a pacif - - '

'So did I kid, seems you're a bad influence!' The romance is over. Dino walks away, doesn't look back, his parting words,

'Don't start sometheeng you can't finish.' Davy nurses his jaw, bends to pick up his mangled spliff – he takes a puff, but the shredded weed falls apart, his mind racked with confusion. All other miners have long since gone, except one who passes, watching the spaced out hippy's solitary figure, imploring the dark cosmos to hear him out,

'Screw you man! Is that all you saw down there man?! Is that all?! You'll never know man, never know the real truth, because you're a cop out man, you don't know the real mother earth man...where the dragon sleeps tonight...the white rabbit man, he knows...ask Alice man...she fell down that hole too, every kid knows except you...because you can't see where it's at man!'

Alice had got so much into the way of expecting nothing but out-of-the-way things to happen, that it seemed quite dull and stupid for life to go on in the common way.
  Lewis Carroll, Alice's Adventures in Wonderland

Davy finds solace in his bedroom sanctuary, tries to sleep in, now that the mine is on lockdown due to the strike. His eyes seem to focus and refocus on the bedroom walls, bedecked with posters and prints, *Creams' Disraeli Gears psychedelic vinyl cover, Jefferson Airplane – White Rabbit, Easy Rider movie poster, a colour newspaper pull-out poster of the Beatles*...but he soon snaps out of it. He hears a gnawing sound at the end of his bed...he jumps up and finds Dusty the poodle eating his wacky-baccy and spent spliffs from an ash-tray.

'Oh man!' Peggy calls up the stairs,

'Davy, y'alright? Is Dusty with you?' He grabs the poodle, jolts his knee as Dusty smiles back with the weirdest canine stare.

'Yeh sis, just mellowing...think I'll take her for a walk...seeing the strike's on n'all.' Peggy thinks she must have misheard her brother and replies,

'*You're* taking Dusty out? Is everything OK?'

****

Outside the colliery gates, Davy and Dusty join his crew, standing with scores of picketing miners. Grady and his pit-bull terrier pace close by. Grady's eyes focus on Davy, whilst his pit-bull's gaze fixates on Dusty. Taffy's in a khaki Boar War regimental uniform, courtesy of local pawn shop. Big Hewett turns to Davy and tells him,

'The kid was a loose cannon - - '

'Yeah, big balls, taking a swing at you like that.' Taffy says.

'Wanted a refund did 'e on his grand tour?' Big Hewett asks.

'Look, let's just forget it, okay man?' Davy replies.

'Too much aggression, these young un's, no respect see, hasn't been through a war,' Taffy says.

Davy looks at Taffy's uniform, 'And you have I s'pose? Burma wasn't it?'

'The little I-ti prick isn't worth beating yourself up about.' Taffy suggests.

'Jesus, would you guys not use that phrase?' Davy asks.

'Okay, 'Die' isn't worth beating yourself up about.' Taffy rephrases.

Davy gives up, tugs Dusty's lead to go walkies.

'Shit, forget it man!' Big Hewett pats Davy on the shoulder and says,

'We're just trying to sympathise here Davy.'

'I don't need your sympathy man – it was a bad trip, I need time to...Dusty needs a walk.'

All eyes linger on the poodle as they notice his weird 5-mile stare, sitting in a puddle.

'Trouble passing water has she?' Taffy says biting his lip. Big Hewett gives them an education,

'They're actually water dogs, if you didn't know lads. The Kraut word 'Pudel', means paddle, might explain it.' Davy holds his arms up in despair, yanking Dusty out of the water.

'What? Now you're a friggin' dog shrink? She's fine man.'

Even the Pit-Bull looks freaked by the 'far out' lunch on a lead. Davy's about to leave.

'Anyway, the kid had no future here, we all know that.' Taffy states.

'*He* had no future?! Look around you man, this mother's going tits up!' Davy says.

'Never seen you this uptight before – the kid really got to you didn't 'e? What else did he say?' Big Hewett asks.

Davy feels guilty, now seeing the 'tired old' crew Dino described. He sighs, stays silent. Big Hewett tries to comfort him, asking,

'How many strikes have we seen over the years, eh? This'll pass Davy.'

Davy adds, 'Like the years, eh? I can smell the mothballs already man.'

One of the miners, perched high up on a wall, puts a loudhailer to his transistor radio – Radio One news bulletin blares out from the heavens. *'A small group of Nottingham miners working at what's been called the 'Pit of Nations', employing migrants from the British Colonies and Commonwealth, have formed a co-operative to buy their mine...'*

Davy recalls Ma Hewett's prophecy, *'You'll hear the voice from above...it will guide you...it's going to be Sunny.'*

Davy looks at the overcast, grey sky, still can't figure that. He thinks, *Maybe it'll brighten up?*

The news finishes and *'Something in the Air' by Thunderclap Newman* plays.

****

Moments later, union officials and picketing miners gather outside the Colliery Main Office. Inside, Bevan approaches Tarrant. Through the partition window, Davy is visible waiting in the corridor. Tarrant turns to Bevan and asks,

'Who is he?'

'Davy Johnson, wants a word, you'll know him, lost two of his crew, took over from Pennant.'

'From who? Oh, right.'

Davy enters with Dusty, on a lead, 'sleepwalking'. Valma's stood by a filing cabinet in an adjoining office, sorting documents. She looks up, smiles, walks over, and starts fussing with the dog.

'She's all wet.'

Davy shares his canine expertise, 'Yeah, they're water dogs y' know, pretty cool...Germans call them 'paddles'.' Valma looks impressed,

'I didn't know that. Is she yours?'

'Me sister's – and mine I s'pose, belonged to me mum.'

Tarrant intervenes, stares at the open filing cabinet and Valma, lingering on her cleavage. She straightens herself from petting the poodle,

'I best get on.' She leaves them to it. Tarrant comments acidically,

'So – not by choice then? The bitch? Not a mascot you'd take to picket lines? No, you didn't strike me as y' normal miner.'

'Normally, I don't usually strike,' Davy replies.

'No, you just supply the entertainment 'round 'ere don't you? Not your typical NUM radical.'

'A numb-nut? Not me man, mining's in the family blood. 'Radical' is what I'd call closing mines from Dulais to Swansea valley man.' These men don't like each other, Tarrant justifies his actions,

'Closing mines is never easy. All comes down to economics.' He walks over to the window, looks outside at the union members, 'Your Union's had copies of the reports.' Efficient, thorough, in black shiny shoes, Davy's polar opposite,

'Coal bags versus body bags? Tough call man.' Davy replies.

'What's hard for me is managing a working mine that's not working,' Tarrant says.

'What about safety man? And loyalty to y' workforce? Some of these miners have been here all their life man, that doesn't concern you?'

Davy's had subtler moments, now Tarrant's expensive suit seems to define him as he spells it out,

'Loyalty?! You think your and our customers care if their anthracite comes from Merthyr, the Midlands or Mao Tse China? Come winter, when their coal-sheds are empty, and their kids are freezing, ask them. Davy mulls that for a beat. 'Yeah, bugger isn't it, managing a mine.'

Davy looks across to the militants outside, uglier, louder than before, bearing support placards. Tarrant's diatribe cranks up a notch,

'As for sympathy? That comes at a price my friend. Oh, you'll get their warm support alright for about...three weeks...maybe a month, then they'll get theirs from a sack of cheap commie coal – 'cos that's how long you've got!'

Tarrant ushers Davy and Dusty out, starts closing the door, but Davy reacts, jams his sandal against it, even surprises himself. His eyes fix Tarrant dead on as he offers an idea,

'What about co-operative coal?' Tarrant laughs and replies,

'Oh, so you 'eard it too did you? On the radio? You mean, run this place yourself?'

In the back office, Valma listens as she arranges a flower vase. Davy looks as fazed as Tarrant does at his proposal, but nods all the same. Outside the window, Tarrant watches Davy's crew appear, Taffy straightens his khaki uniform and adjusts his eye-patch in the window reflection.

'With that lot?' Tarrant comments, as if it's a joke. The conversation is over. Tarrant pushes the poodle out and shuts the door with finality, but Davy's knee doubles as a human doorstop.

'I've a committed crew - - ' Davy insists.

'Committed'? Maybe they should be, tstch, your phrase - - ' Tarrant replies.

'Four, maybe five - - ' Davy says.

'Can't be done, sorry.' Tarrant replies.

'Then I'll recruit more?!' Davy suggests.

'Hope you've got a hippy commune, you'll need twenty, at least.' Tarrant informs him.

'Twenty?! What about those Nottingham miners? They managed - - '

THE PLEDGE

Davy checks the note Valma gave him under a street lamp-post light, Avery's address is closer to the mine than he expected. In fact, its rear garden must back onto the east section of the spent mine shafts.

As Davy is about to knock on the door, it opens, and a doctor with his medical bag leaves. Davy greets him with a smile and brushes past to see Mrs Avery in the doorway. Her stick-thin, frail body steps back to close the door, but being virtually blind, she traps Davy's accident-prone knee. She calls out,

'I'm so sorry doctor, did you forget something?'

'Mrs Avery, I'm not the doctor, I'm Davy. Davy Johnson, a friend of your husband's.'

'Oh, I see...it's a bit late for visitors, he's not well you see.'

'I'm sorry to hear that...I didn't know he was...what if I came back tomorrow? Say in the morning?'

Mrs Avery considers the precious time and the night ahead,

as her husband calls out,

'Who is it Gwynn? I can hear you chatting and a male voice?'

'It's Davy Johnson, a friend of yours,' Mrs Avery informs.

'Well let the poor fellow in, he'll catch a death in that draft.'

Mrs Avery takes Davy through to their bedroom. Old Man Avery is fading fast, but Davy's presence ignites a twinkle. Lucky is settled by his bedside. Mrs Avery comments,

'He tried taking the dog back to its owner but nobody was home. That's two new friends he's made this week.'

Avery's voice, though weak, is laced with passion. He hoists himself up from his pillows and looks at Davy, as if inspecting a new recruit. He speaks slowly, conserving energy to relay his vital message,

'I's hoping I'd see you. Gwynn, the suitcase. Could you fetch it please?'

In the warm glow of a bedside table lamp, Davy is captivated by a framed photo on the wall. Mr and Mrs Avery in their late twenties perhaps, standing in front of *two isolated columns of rock,* against a windswept, barren landscape.

Mrs Avery squints, notices Davy's interest in the photo and tells him,

'That's Adam and Eve. We found them on our honeymoon, just after the Great War. Time seemed to stand still back then.' Davy asks,

'Yeh...something about them. Where was that?'

'Tryfan, in the Cambrian Mountains. Legend has it that whoever can leap from one rock to the other will find eternal happiness.' She opens the wardrobe to retrieve the suitcase from behind a rack of hanging clothes.

'Man...that's one 'giant leap for mankind' without going to the moon.'

She smiles at that.

'Did you make it?' he asks.

As she's about to answer, Old Man Avery interrupts, 'Gwynn, what you doing?!'

From inside a wardrobe, she extracts an *old leather suitcase*. Davy looks concerned and asks,

'You're not going anywhere tonight are you?' Gwynn gazes heavenward and whispers to Davy,

'No love, not tonight...unless *he* has other plans.'

Old Man Avery overhears that and proclaims,

'*'He's'* got bugger all to do with it!'

'He wasn't this profane when I married him - - ' Gwynn responds.

'*'He* hadn't been through a war either,' Avery states.

'If this is a bad time I can - - ' Davy says, but Avery cuts him off,

'It won't get any better lad, but you could change that. Pass me the good book would you?'

Davy can't see a bible anywhere, but Gwynn points to a book on the bedside table. Davy picks it up, *'Dylan Thomas – Anthology of Poetry'*.

'The *'Good book'*? Davy questions.

'Good enough for me, one kindred voice, unscarred by centuries of clerics. Page seventy nine I'm at, if you wouldn't mind?' Davy looks at Gwynn, is he expected to read it? Gwynn tries to focus as she explains,

'I haven't been able to for a good many years now, he misses that.'

She puts her delicate hand on Davy's wrist, places the suitcase by his feet and tells him,

'It's an unspoken pledge you're making, you know that don't you? He trusts you...you see...this has been his life.'

Davy feels the suitcase by his leg. He rubs his knee and settles the large book upon it, like he's under oath. He glances at Gwynn, eyes searching. 'Man...this is heavy.'

In her milky-blind orbs, he finds resolve, holds the book with purpose, senses some karmic fate fuse has been lit as he begins to read it aloud,

'Do not go gentle into that good night...rage, rage against the dying of the light...'

As Davy continues, Avery's eyes burn fiercely with passion as he mouths the words, almost imperceptibly,

'A-u-r C-y-m-r-u.' *('W-e-l-s-h G-o-l-d')*

Davy hears Avery mutter and stops reading.

'Sorry? Was there something?' Davy asks.

Avery's hand slowly drops to touch the black labrador, as he speaks to himself in Welsh,

'Lwcus.' *(Lucky)*

Avery is resting. Gwynn nods to Davy, a tacit '*thankyou*'. Davy looks at another framed photo on a tallboy dresser of Old Man Avery, a young handsome beau in uniform, standing next to Gwynn in a floral summer dress. Davy lets the old boy sleep, places the book by his side and leaves with the suitcase.

****

Later that night, Davy retires to his bedroom and places Avery's suitcase on the bed. He shuts the door, but it jams. He looks baffled and checks that there's nothing wedged in the doorway... then he notices a thin crack in the wall above the door frame. He curses to himself, knowing it's an indication of some subsidence which he can't deal with right now.

He pushes the metal sliders apart on the suitcase, releasing the catches, which spring up. He hesitates before opening the lid, not knowing what to expect... Inside, he finds a sealed letter and carefully unfolds four meticulously drawn geological maps of the Welsh Valleys – each poster-sized, with a number code. In a side compartment, by the hinges, he discovers a small tobacco pouch. He opens it but can't see anything inside...he tips it up over the map... *GRAINS OF WELSH GOLD* scatter over the topographical valley landscape.

'Holy shit.' He opens Avery's letter to find a key...he can hear the old man's voice as he reads it,

'If you were expecting some old war souvenirs, I'm sorry to disappoint you. You're probably wondering about the key? If you check the map marked *'WFDR 2'*, grid reference D 4, you'll find a fall-out shelter.'

Davy checks the maps and finds *'WFDR 1'* then *'WFDR 2'* – the one referred to. He gently unfolds the map to find, in its top centre margin, the title: *'DUNKIRK RETREAT, THE OUTER LIMITS'*, every feature painstakingly drafted: *'Concorde Roadway, DR40 Seam, Burma, Arras, Dieppe etc.'*, all identified by numerous codes.

'Holy shit man!' He finger-traces the route from the fall-out shelter in Avery's back garden to the mine itself. He hears Valma's voice, *'That's the sad part, he moved four times, I mean at his age'*. Davy slowly shakes his head in disbelief,

'Your own *private entrance*, you dug your own private...' Davy lights up a joint to calm his anxious, excited state, before he absorbs the full import of what he's looking at.

'You're blowing my mind man! You sly old fox.' Davy's hand starts shaking as he continues reading the letter – now the old man seems to be really speaking to him,

'Dunkirk Retreat meets the Outer Limits' boundary on a fault line that runs...' Davy's nail tracks the fault line which runs beneath the pit head gates and colliery main office to an area marked with a ringed dot. His finger pressure causing the map paper to vibrate the gold sprinkles, making them dance in the light.

'Jesus man...it's right under their bloody noses.'

1969

Next day, Taffy and Big Hewett arrive outside their local ABC Castle Super Cinema in Merthyr Tydfil and stand on the corner entrance, looking down both street approaches for Davy. They look at the billboard poster outside: *'The Italian Job'* starring *Michael Caine*. Taffy takes out his chain pocket watch, checks the time and comments,

'He's late.'

Big Hewett looks at the poster and remarks,

'This'll cheer him up won't it? 'The Italian Job'.'

'Well, it was his idea. We've bugger all else to do today and it might just 'elp him forget that foetus with a crew-cut,' Taffy remarks.

'My canary won't forget 'im in a hurry, after three baths.'

Davy arrives, breathless, clutching a book.

The crew enter the foyer and somehow Taffy shrinks and squat-walks as they join a small queue by the kiosk. The kiosk lady, in her fifties, sporting an ABC blazer with a white nylon blouse, adjusts her 'Cat eye' glasses and studies the curious rag-bag trio as Big Hewett pays and asks for,

'Two adults and one 'miner' please love.' The woman looks over her counter, down at Taffy, who smiles and waves.

'No school today then?' Taffy shakes his head as Davy holds up his book and says,

'I've got his homework.'

She breathes in heavily and warns them,

'Any trouble from you lot and you're out.' She looks across to her cinema manager for endorsement. Barry, a portly effete man in his fifties, is standing to her left with a mug of tea, left hand poised mid-dunk with a Rich Tea biscuit. He puts his tea-mug on a filing cabinet, jaw clenched, and inhales, inflating his blazer and dickie-bow to look like a bad ass.

Later, inside the auditorium, a meagre matinee audience is spread out in the stalls. The crew are settled in the middle, away from other patrons – unaware of the acerbic elderly lady, Nell, who they know from their village, and who has shuffled in behind them.

On the screen, the post-heist memorable scene. Mini Cooper S's tear along an Italian route, lining up their wheels to mount trailing metal ramps onto a speeding truck. It's at this precise moment that Davy's euphoric connection with gold translates into an auto-reflex. He produces a white handkerchief and opens it in front of Taffy and Big Hewett, revealing the yellow piece of gleaming 'grit'. They look down bemusedly.

A little later...Davy is trying hard to convince them...

'But that could have fallen out of the old boy's head,' Big Hewett states. Davy replies,

'There were specks too man. I thought I was dreaming it after I fell through the rabbit hole - - '

'The what?' Big Hewett asks. Davy brushes that aside,

'Nothing man, just a term...I remember the kid next to me, couldn't breathe 'cos of the dust man, and I remember brushing it off...yellow, fine grit...didn't think anything of it at the time.'

'You're not using the right shampoo,' Taffy quips. Davy leans forward, holding the book and patting it,

'Look, seriously, I've been doing some reading, Avery's not the only one, there's a history of gold prospectors who've - - '

'Got dandruff?' Taffy says.

' - - who've searched for it! Welsh gold!' Davy insists. Taffy responds,

'Hey, now you mention it, I remember the historic event...*The Great British Gold Rush*! (In Welsh) Ma' 'da ni gystal siawns i ffindo hwnnw â châl ffwc 'da Tom Jones' *(We've as much chance of finding that as being propositioned by Tom Jones).*

Big Hewett puckers his lips and starts preening himself in an imaginary mirror, saying,

'Ooh, I don't know...'

Nell, the old lady sitting behind 'shushes' them loudly. Davy crouches forward, whispers to his crew.

'Look guys, you think this is a joke? Like everyone thought the old man was? Well, so did I man, when he visited me in hospital, waving his freak flag high, I thought Avery was as mad as a hatter. Now I know different. I'm just as mad as him, mad to live, mad to love and mad to discover. He has a system, just like my old man had for the football pools, never altered it man,'cos he knew, he knew man that every week some dude would win the friggin' jackpot man.'

'So did my old man. He had a system, a formula, but he never won anything, just like yours. We'd have known, right, if 'e had?' Big Hewett asks.

'Sure man, I think dad won twenty pounds once, he got close... but the thing is man, they never gave up, just like Old Man Avery – he has maps man, proof...which we'll need to study before we start digging.'

'Hold on there, Davy, just hold on a bleedin' mo', maps aren't proof, they are Avery's theories – of a *coal* mine, *coal*. They don't prove anything until it's found. So, before we gayly skip into Alice-land here, we're *coal-miners*, not *gold prospectors*.'

'You're right Hew', we're not, 'cos we've already found it!' (He points at the minute nugget and holds up the book) 'I got this from the library, listen to this (he flips to a bookmarked page) 'Au', that's the chemical symbol for gold, but get this man, it's Atomic Number is 79!'

'Your house number? That's one hell of a coincidence.' Taffy states.

'Yes, and that's all it is.' Big Hewett responds. Davy has more Zen mind-benders to reveal and tells them,

'Ok, let's just say that is one cosmic chance of colossal proportions man, then this next fact will blow you away, it's Atomic Weight is, you're not gonna believe this brother...it's... 1 9 6 9. That my friend is here and now, *us* in *this* moment in time.

Underwhelmed silence, except for the film's soundtrack, as Taffy and Big Hewett dwell on that. Davy's philosophising continues, 'Let your minds be parachutes man, they won't work unless they're open. The first number is gold and it's screwed to my front door man. Destiny came knocking and found me home. The other numbers are speaking to us all man, right now.'

Big Hewett is mellowing and responds with some caution,

'P'raps we can hear them now, but not as clearly as you – 'cos of the soundtrack?' Taffy nods.

'Avery once told me it was all about numbers...wasn't sure what he meant at the time but one, nine, six, nine is telling me that this is a new dawn for us, of men on the moon, of Concorde soaring high above us and...and Woodstock man! They're playing our song and we've just got to get it together!' Davy states his case. Taffy and Big Hewett are considering it all and their silence seems louder than the movie.

'I know this all sounds a little crazy, but no crazier than what we do every day,' Davy insists.

'But what about all the other experts, R and D's geologists... reports and surveys the NCB's had over the years?' Big Hewett asks.

'And how many good mines have they shut over the years? How many so called rich seams didn't make a year? They're looking for coal not gold man,' Davy explains, as on screen, the coach is climbing through the Alps with the gold bullion. Taffy has a question and asks,

'Okay, I get that. But say if it's kosher, how come Old Man Avery tells you? A complete bloody stranger?'

'Yeah Davy, why not keep this treasure trove to himself?' Big Hewett asks. Davy gives a sigh and tells them,

'Because, he's an old man, an old man who's only got himself and his dreams – dreams he once shared with his brother.'

Nell, behind them, leans forward, tuts and thumps Davy's seat. Big Hewett whispers as loud as he can over the film, as Michael Caine's crew sing in celebration, ascending the snaking mountain pass,

'And where's he now...his brother?' Asks Big Hewett. Davy replies, keeping it positive,

'Look man, all I know is that they spent a lifetime together, searching and...'

'Now it's our turn?' Taffy says.

They pass the tiny nugget around, which glints in the half light from the cinema screen. Nell observes their queer antics and crotch-level fumblings. Taffy scrutinises it and comments,

'Could be iron pyrites in this light.'

'Old Man Avery might be many things but he's no fool man,' Davy tells them.

'Ow far back from the roadway does the old boy reckon it is?' says Big Hewett.

'Dunkirk Retreat? Half a mile roughly, according to his map.' Davy says.

'With shit for a roof,' Taffy says. Davy agrees,

'Sure man, the props are shot, we'll 'ave to replace 'em to get to the vein. And that, when we find it – according to Avery's notes, is embedded in quartz, galena and sandstone,' Davy says.

'Gonna need a lot of tungsten rippers,' Taffy says.

'And a lot of luck,' Big Hewett concludes.

On the screen, that cliffhanger ending... Michael Caine and his crew watch the gold bullion stack, slipping further and further to the back of the teetering coach, with them at the opposite end, balancing on the mountain edge fulcrum...Michael Caine says, *'Hang on a minute lads, I've got a great idea.'*

Taffy and Big Hewett look to each other for endorsement as the credits roll, Big Hewett says,

'Well...maybe it's worth a recce?' Davy grins from ear to ear and hugs them both – overseen by Nell, seated behind them.

After the film, the three of them exit into the foyer. Nell is chatting to the Kiosk lady and both look across suspiciously at the crew as they enter the toilets.

Inside, standing at the urinals, Davy converses with his two-man crew.

'Nobody must tell a soul outside of this circle, total secrecy man, that goes for wives and y' ma too.

'And y' sister, she's no stranger to gossip.' Big Hewett says. Reaction of 'mission impossible' from Taffy as he shakes his head and states,

'Lyn could find truffles with 'er nose.'

'Ma'll see it in the tea leaves.' Big Hewett says.

'Then make her coffee in the mornings like I told you. I'm serious man, in the current climate, if anyone gets wind of this we're screwed,' Davy says.

'If this pans out – pardon the pun – a fever could hit this region like we've never seen,' Big Hewett comments.

Taffy produces a Swiss army knife and levers out a blade which glints as he proposes,

'Then we'll swear an oath...a blood oath of allegiance!'

'Let's not get too carried away man.' Davy says.

'No, I think that's champion, with what's at stake, it'll bond us together,' Big Hewett replies.

'We need to call ourselves something, like the Templar Knights, y'know, something chivalric?' Taffy suggests.

'What about...'The Crew Who Knew'? Big Hewett proudly proposes.

'That's not a name man, that's...like a book title,' Davy replies.

'A bit 'novel' I know but - - ' replies Big Hewett.

'Mine Gold - Men! M-G-M,' Taffy suggests.

"Mien Gold?' Sounds like Nazi stolen treasure,' Big Hewett says.

'MGM? Now we're movie moguls,' Davy says.

'I've got one...The Davy Johnson Trio,' Taffy suggests.

'Yeah man, cool, like Roy Budd...all we need is a piano,' Davy replies. Big Hewett looks inspired and says,

'No we don't boys, we've got our own voice, we call ourselves 'Deep Harmony'...like the hymn.'

Somehow that strikes a spiritual chord with the crew.

'That's choice man, it transcends like...when I hear 'Rock of Ages' sang in church, it connects with Gaia man,' Davy says.

'I like the sound of that...Deep Harmony,' Taffy concludes.

'It's Crosby, Stills and Nash man,' Davy says.

Ritualistic nods as Taffy cuts his palm...a vein of blood oozes. He passes the knife to Big Hewett. Davy's next and looking anxious. One by one, they press their palms together, then overlay their hands.

'All for one...and one for all!' Davy says as they all join in.

Outside the toilet entrance, Nell peers through and sees them all holding hands. She looks repulsed, her suspicions confirmed, and as the crew disengage to exit past, they all nod in unison and greet her,

'Nell.' She stands rooted to the spot and spits.

THE FALL-OUT SHELTER

Early evening, the 'Deep Harmony' trio approach Avery's house in heavy rain. The colliery winch-wheel's colossal shadow looms in the background as if it were a giant garden climbing frame planted in Avery's back yard. Outside the terraced cottage, an ambulance is parked, two medics are by the rear doors, pulling out a folding trolley-bed in the pouring rain. Davy and his crew watch from the opposite side of the street. Through the front room window, Davy recognises the doctor comforting Mrs Avery. Two others, either relatives or neighbours, are present as the medics join them. Moments later, the medics emerge through the front door with a black-bagged corpse on the trolley.

Davy shakes his head slowly and begins to leave. Big Hewett asks,

'Where the hell are you going?'

'Home. Show some respect man. This is not the time.' Davy replies.

'But we're here getting drenched 'cos of you and you're here 'cos of 'im,' Taffy says.

'Isn't this what he would 'ave wanted? I mean...all those years, 'im and his brother? The way I see it is that they've handed us the baton and somehow, by whatever means, it's up to us now – it's up to *Deep Harmony* to finish the race,' Big Hewett proclaims.

'Jesus, spare me the speech man...it's just...I would have liked him to have been there,' Davy replies.

'He has been there, that's the point. You said you made some sort of pledge with him, right? Well, we've made an oath with you to see it through.'

Davy takes out a joint and lights it, inhales deeply, realises their analysis is right.

'Ok...I'm cool man...just let me think...'

Davy starts walking, the crew follow him, through an alleyway that leads to the back of the terraced cottages where they locate Avery's back garden, part-lit by the rear kitchen fluorescent light. An allotment vegetable patch runs from the back of the cottage to the fall-out shelter sited close to the back fence. Davy can see movement in the kitchen, Mrs Avery at the sink with a helper.

'Perhaps I should go in there and say...' Davy suggests.

'Say what exactly Davy? It's not like you'll be amongst relatives and old friends now is it? I forgot though, you go back days don't you?' Big Hewett says.

'I just feel I ought to say something,' Davy says as he looks at the key and map he's holding.

'What exactly? *I'm sorry? I didn't want to disturb you but as I've got my own shed key, would it be convenient for me and the boys - -*' Big Hewett responds. Davy reflects, deep in thought, saying, 'I have her consent...it was Gwynn who gave me the suitcase and thanked me.'

'There you go then,' Big Hewett says.

'Why don't you call in tomorrow and pay your respects?' Taffy says.

'We all could for that matter – but right now we're here and there's business to attend to and as it happens, Deep Harmony have a special guest pass.'

They quietly open the back gate and find the fall-out shelter door-lock visible, faintly illuminated by the convex corrugated metal roof. Davy inserts the key and unlocks the shelter...the rusty door hinges creak as he steps inside, down a step followed quickly by Big Hewett and Taffy who close the door behind them. A sloshing sound greets them as Davy flicks on his torch to find that they are standing in a foot of water on concrete steps that descend below the water line between two concrete ledges either side. On the ledges are stacked railway timber sleepers that fit between the ledge recesses covering the passage.

'Shit!' Davy says. Taffy and Big Hewett turn on their torches.

'And 'ow d'you propose we do a recce? Phone Jacques Cousteau?!' Taffy says.

'Should've brought me trunks, didn't mention he 'ad a swimming pool in his garden,' Big Hewett says.

'Old Man 'Auric Goldfinger' could afford it couldn't he?!' Taffy proclaims. Deep Harmony are not sounding *that* harmonious right now as Davy's short-fuse response indicates,

'Jesus man! Okay, okay! So, he didn't mention the flooding but... (he shines his torch on the map)...his map shows it's a Miocene Caenozoic layer.'

'Meaning?' Taffy asks.

'Oh, don't encourage 'im, we had double chemistry at the flicks,' Big Hewett comments.

'Meaning it's close to the water table and if you hadn't noticed man, it's been pissing down recently...*but* it's porous. Sure, it'll flood alright, but it'll drain.' Outside, the rain of a thousand drum-sticks beats down on the tin roof.

'Not tonight it won't,' Taffy comments.

'You've gotta put up with some rain man, if you want that rainbow with that pot of gold.'

'Best we give it a day or so to ease off,' Big Hewett suggests.

'It'll be an all-nighter, just say we're at the pub,' Davy suggests.

'Or scuba diving?' Taffy quips.

'And if it becomes a regular thing – which it will, from what we've gleaned so far, what's our excuse gonna be?' Big Hewett asks.

'It's cool, we make out like we're doing something constructive man, with the strike 'n all, something to occupy us on those nights that sounds feasible,' Davy suggests.

'Well, you can join me for a rugby warm-up for this Trelewis lark I got roped into,' Big Hewett suggests.

Taffy responds, 'No good, that'll be over by the weekend, we need a more long term - - '

Davy interjects, ' - - It's gotta be credible, something believable that Deep Harmony could...(he has a eureka moment)...bleeding obvious isn't it? Choir practice.'

Taffy and Big Hewett exit the shelter and start singing the hymn *Rock of Ages'* in low tones...meanwhile Davy finds a metal box on a high shelf which he opens...

Davy joins the mini choir outside, all sing in harmony as they lock up and leave through the back gate. Big Hewett pauses and looks back at the challenge ahead, saying,

'So much for a rear entry.' Davy has an epiphany and imitates Michael Caine from the last scene in *The Italian Job*.

''Hang on a minute lads, I've got a great idea'. Who said we're taking the old girl from behind? This is a crusade man...Deep Harmony is taking the missionary position.'

Davy senses a presence...then a something prodding against his leg. He looks down to find Lucky looking back up at him. 'Hey man, he must have got out when the ambulance arrived.'

The crew watch the dog walk away purposefully, then stop and look back at the crew as if to follow... The crew exchange glances... Davy watches Lucky and feels impelled by some extra-mundane force to follow. Big Hewett gestures, thumbing behind him and calls out, 'Now where you off to? Your place is back that way?'

Davy calls out, 'So is Pennant's man...don't you see?'

The crew conspire a look and reply in unison, 'No.'

Davy pauses briefly to enlighten them, 'We gotta follow man... don't really know why but...I feel it'd be un-Lucky not to.'

'THEY CALL ME MR TIBBS'

Along William Street's terraced cottages and into Wood Street, the stalking cluster of miners keep pace with Lucky who walks around a corner and disappears in to the night. The crew squint at the dimly lit row of cottages ahead, many abandoned dwellings with fractured frontages, yielding to subsidence. Outside one of the condemned small houses sits Lucky...his dark silhouette just visible, motionless.

The crew approach...Lucky affords them a *'Glad you could make it'* look , as the mystified crew arrive. Big Hewett slowly shakes his head,

'What in God's name are we doing here Davy boy?' Davy's about to answer but is interrupted by the front door opening...a match ignites...just one arm and hand in an assured movement, touching a spliff held in metal pincers for a hand. It glints, fixed to a prosthetic arm, belonging to a lean Jamaican in his late 40s, Tibsy. He scrutinises the assembled guests in the rain and speaks loudly,

'We're all here for a reason my friend.'

The crew step back...a sort of reflex action directed at the two white eyes and smoke-glow emanating from the dark figure in the porch way. Tibsy switches on a hallway light, which seems to create a Kirlian haze around him...steps forward and, with his good left arm, pats the dog in disbelief,

'The Old Man's old haunt...you come back to see the ol' place? Mi sey mi see you just last week, how is you now dead?' The Jamaican takes a deep, sorrowful breath, rubs his short curly hair as if massaging his mind to ease the loss of an old companion. Then squats down level with Lucky and strokes him.

A sublime intervention of purpose inexplicably shared by all present makes the crew uneasy yet euphoric, as if Old Man Avery's spirit had accessed their very souls. Taffy adjusts his clothing, stretching his neck and shoulders as if his body and mind need a moment to reassess being in the scheme of things. Davy 's first to respond as he stares at Lucky and looks down at the one-armed Jamaican,

'Man...I know you...the black dynamite dude the old man spoke about...this must be Avery's old place man...you must be Tibsy?' The Jamaican studies Davy's lips, strains to hear, then stops stroking the dog, looks up and stands, straightening himself. And with feigned indignation, addresses Davy and his crew,

'Back home they call me *Mister Tibbs*.' He studies their stern acceptance then bursts out laughing,

'And back home – it was a whole lot dryer too my friends!' Lucky brushes past Tibsy and walks inside, watched by all four.

Tibsy looks at the crew,

'Some is born to lead, some's born to follow.' Tibsy lets out a roar of laughter and pats Davy on the back as the crew enter, 'So, the ol' man have you diggin' for that treasure too now?'

Sometime later, the crew are huddled together drinking rum in a small back kitchen. Davy shares a joint with Tibsy as Taffy and Big Hewett gaze out the window, beyond a garden shed where, in the distance, the tops of two vertical wooden posts can be seen in the fading evening light. Davy notices a framed photo of a young black boy on the window ledge, holding a football,

'Is that your boy?'

'Sidney junior that be...and me being Sid senior and one of the first black miners you folks saw here back then, they decided on calling me Mister Tibbs as the only black face they'd known was that Hollywood star Sidney Poitier in 'The Heat of the Night'...and as he was a cool and sophisticated *detective*...oh my, yessir...Oh mean, that brother kicked some white ass like never before... Lord did he just! So they reasoned I'd have a nose for *detecting* where to plant their sticks of dynamite...and I got good – real good...my investigations of seams, geological structures, types of explosives...Old Man Avery knew me when I had it real sweet.'

He takes a swig of rum and ponders a deep rooted thought,

'Them jokes came later...those blackies 'll give their right arm for a job. The ol' man and his brother were a class act my friends, after Ora, my wife, left me and the boy, Avery let me live here... (pats his false arm) got Mr Tibbs some steel fingers and thumb, so I helped them dig out back...' Tibsy points at the window...

Davy's eyes follow the crew's far reaching focus, fixated on the wooden posts and is confused...

'Where man? What d'you mean you dug? Out there man?'

Tibsy recounts the event with a flurry of hand actions that seem to reanimate his story,

'The first tunnel did not go deep enough my friend...or far enough for Avery and Dougie...the route on his map the *'First Approach'* he called it...*WFDR 1* kept caving in...again and again, month after month, like the Lord above was trying tell him *'This ain't the way my friend...'* so we shored it up as best we could...with one strong arm and steel claw... You see, when Avery lost his brother it's like the Lord took my arm and spoke to me...*'You best stay up top now and take care of your boy!'* So, I vowed never to return...and just like me, the digging finally gave up the ghost right under that rugby pitch by them far posts.'

Big Hewett's eyes widen, 'Jesus...I'm playing on that pitch this weekend...d'you think - - '

Tibsy pats Big Hewett and assures him,

'Don't you worry my friend, it will be fine. Sidney Junior plays football there all the time...as he hates rugby...I just tell him to stay away from them far posts. They've played rugby there on many occasion in the past...when it's dry.'

Taffy contributes to Big Hewett's concern, 'Yes, but not for a long while and it's been soddin' raining non-stop for weeks hasn't it?'

Tibsy enquires, 'Then why not wait 'til the good Lord's beautiful sun shines down on us all once again my friend?'

Davy informs him, 'Cos the Trelewis Colliery suits with their *'Get Tomorrow, Today'* bullshit wanna kick our asses man, for the Royal Prince's side-show.'

THE PITCH

A collective canopy of umbrellas are clumped together, ready for the 10.30 morning kick-off, behind the pitch border spectator area. The relentless rain eases as the local colliery, in almost matching tatty sports kit, step out on to the pitch with the pristine blue bedecked outfits of the Trelewis Colliery team right on their tail. Cheers ring out from scores of miners with their sons, daughters, and wives in support, looking on. On an elevated verge opposite, a Land Rover bearing the Royal Coat of Arms discretely pulls in and parks, followed by the Prince's royal blue Aston Martin DB6 Volante convertible, with registration plates: EBY 776J.

Grady and his Pit Bull almost rub shoulders with two Trelewis officials. One of which is Clancy, early 40s, an arch enemy whose career path and future with the new age colliery seems to exude from his every fibre. He stands with a white collar colleague, confidently detached in expensive raincoats, as they observe their team coach, exercising a pre-emptive starter strategy for their players. Grady clocks the blue Aston as he leans across to Clancy and comments,

'Need more than matching socks and shirts to impress our Royal visitors...thought you'd have some of y'robot tin men out there too as full-backs.'

Clancy responds without turning his head, 'That's far too *tomorrow* Grady...too...shall we say, hi-tech for this place wouldn't you say?'

Davy and Taffy stand at the far end of the pitch as Big Hewett, sporting Taffy's regimental khaki shorts, comes into view from behind one of his team's fly half players. Taffy gives him the thumbs up as the referee gathers the two collieries together and flips a coin. The game kicks off underscored by a cacophony of tactical yells and bellowing from clusters of miners.

Davy's view of Tibsy's terraced house in the distance gradually becomes shrouded in mist as the light seems to be fading...and as Davy glances back towards the goal posts, he sees a flash of white as a rabbit disappears through a hole on the fog slimed pitch.

Minutes into the game's first half, the Trelewis side are in possession of the ball as Big Hewett's team defend the goal line area near Davy and Taffy's vantage point.

One of the opposing team kicks the ball high up from the half-way line beyond the 22 metre line...all eyes watch as a high wind and wisp of fog carries the leather projectile, until it erratically drops to earth and clump-bounces...trickling onto the goal line. Big Hewett is closest...starts to panic...and avoiding the 'shored up' weak ground area, gingerly holds onto the goal posts and, with his outstretched leg in flapping regimental khaki shorts, tries to kick the ball away...and finally succeeds, to the total bemusement of his team and onlookers. What in Hell's name is he up to?

A little later, as the fog begins to thicken, the Trelewis team Captain, the number 10 fly-half, decides to change tactics and exploit the strong wind and low visibility...less traditional Welsh running rugby...more kicking forward and follow...

And so follows that Big Hewett's worst nightmare is about to unfold. As Trelewis' kicking forward tactic inevitably leads to a fumble/knock on, the fog decides to join them near the goal line and the attacking team is awarded a scrum!

At this point I should mention that both teams have sizeable benefits in terms of body mass...in particular Grady's brother, The Eclipse, steps up as our number 8 with Big Hewett, our number 9, ready to grab the ball from under his feet...

As the scrum locks in and starts its mammoth heave, all activity is hidden from the spectators by the fog which has settled in with the interlocked mountain of flesh scrambling over the ball that just landed under their feet...3 meters from the goal post...

Big Hewett stands poised for the ball to emerge from under a mud laden swamp of boots and wedges himself into The Eclipse's underarm in an attempt to shift the heaving bulk away from the touchline...

The Eclipse cranks his head towards Big Hewett, 'Ere?! Which way's you pushin'?!'

Davy and Taffy struggle to see beyond the shroud of thick grey mist as only an amorphic moving mass of miners edge toward the goal posts...

SUDDENLY, a strange, muffled crack rumbles, signaling Big Hewett to extract himself...   The pitch tremors and seems to drown the fading grunts and groans from the scrummage, followed by total silence...

At that moment, and just as mysteriously...the fog slowly subsides to reveal just Big Hewett holding the ball, and his Trelewis opponent, gazing into a LARGE HOLE IN THE GROUND where a two colliery collective of 18 team players were last seen.

TOMORROW'S WORLD

Just after 7.30 p.m., in a deserted lay-by approaching the coal pit, Tarrant is parked in his Jag', next to some sheep grazing on a grassy verge. Inside, a local 'slapper' leans over and unzips his flies. Tarrant reclines back in his leather seat, relaxes, and is about to close his eyes when an immaculate royal blue 10 tonne truck trundles past, with a *'Trelewis Colliery'* logo emblazoned on its trailer, like it just rolled off a production line. Mystified, he checks his walnut dash-board clock and watches the truck intently as it heads towards the pit.

'Someone's working late.'

'That's my job love,' The woman says as she looks up. Tarrant starts the ignition, pulls out of the lay-by, skittering gravel and sheep as he races after it, throwing his passenger about in protest.

'Ere! Where you taking me?'

'Keep your knickers on sweetheart, we're just doing a little sight-seeing,' Tarrant informs her.

'What? At this hour? Nuffink's open?' She says.

'Precisely.'

Moments later at the Pit Head entrance, under a waning moon slathered by fog, Grady with his Pit-Bull terrier and The Eclipse appear through the mist and converse with a select handful of pickets outside the open gates.

Nearby, hidden behind a storage shed, Davy and crew are on standby, furtively observing the clandestine activity. Davy checks his watch.

'Looks like the Kray twins are putting in some overtime.' Big Hewett comments.

'Whatever they're up to man, it's a bad vibe I'm getting. We best chill and sit it out.' Davy says.

Big Hewett's canary tilts his head back and forth and seems intrigued by Taffy's military outfit; a camouflage combat uniform, accented by his eye-patch.

'What regiment is it today? We had the bloody Boer War last week?' Big Hewett asks.

'Special Forces, DPM field dress, Disruptive Pattern Material it stands for, introduced in 1940 and improved 9 years ago...' Taffy educates Big Hewett as he repeatedly pulls the jacket sides together.

'Where are the buttons man?' Davy asks.

'Ah, that's why Stan at the pawn shop let me 'ave it cheaper, should have two epaulette buttons here (taps his chest) and a collar button.'

Taffy pulls out a tin of black polish, starts camouflaging his face

– as if Al Jolson just got conscripted. Davy and Big Hewett look on.

'This could be our finest hour,' Big Hewett says sarcastically.

Taffy extracts a small telescope from his shoulder rucksack, studies the terrain, pans up to the barely visible winch-wheel and back down to ground level. He spies two pickets who are leaving with The Eclipse. Grady, in rock 'n roll glad-rags, stands planted on his turf. His Pit-Bull waits, tethered to a long chain on the gate post. Taffy jollies it up...

'Enemy retreating sa! Just Grady and his Pit-Bull remain on target site,' Taffy reports. Big Hewett takes the telescope to look and as he hands it back, Taffy and Davy notice that the telescope has left a black eye ring. Davy smirks but nobody says a word.

'Great...that's all we need man, is that psycho canine on watch. Anybody got some aniseed balls he could chew?' Davy asks.

'Besides ours you mean?' Big Hewett says. Taffy produces a bag of sweets.

'We could try one of these? Sherbert lemons. I 'eard they make 'em sneeze – throws 'em for a mo' Taffy informs them.

'A mo?' Davy asks.

'And then what?' Big Hewett says.

'Then they chew y' balls off,' Taffy says.

The crew observe headlights approaching the gates as the gleaming blue Leyland haulage truck arrives and almost 'lighthouse' the crew as it rumbles on within two metres of Grady. Davy and his crew lie low, close enough to eavesdrop. The truck driver opens his cabin door and steps down. Clancy, early 40's, looks like he just jumped out of the men's fashion section of a Littlewoods catalogue. Dressed in a crisp blue overall with trouser creases to compliment a chest-pocket stitched logo: *'TRELEWIS COLLIERY'.* He is joined by his passenger, similarly dressed. Grady gives them the once-over and steps back, shielding his eyes as if bedazzled by their presence.

'The Moody Blues are back. I forgot to ask, who does the ironing?' Grady says.

'Piss off Grady,' Clancy responds, as a third passenger, Mr Williams, a thin fifty-something gentleman with clip-board, wearing spectacles and a raincoat, also emerges from the driver cabin and joins them. Grady's pit-bull snarls as Williams keeps his distance.

'So, y' robots still on strike then? Such modern times eh?' Grady says.

'Just teething problems, some new toys need running in,' Clancy smugly replies and Williams agrees.

'And who the hell are you? Mr Fix-it?' Grady asks Williams.

'No, that would be a hybrid Mechanical and Plant Engineer, I'm Glanmore Williams, Mineralogist and Geotechnician.'

'Ah, good 'aving a boffin' around, bit of prestige for the taffy Prince's tour? Seems our mine's more yesterday than tomorrow's world, a bit down market for Charlie boy. Pity he didn't call in on us after the rugby...or fall in like your lot did.'

'God job no one was seriously hurt, that pitch isn't fit for purpose, you need to fence it off,' Clancy replies.

'Bit like your mine then? All that space-age tackle and bugger all to show for it - bloody ironic you needing our coal for window-dressing,' Grady says.

'Well, let's hope it's better than the last lot we paid you for.' Clancy replies as Williams consults his clipboard notes and comments,

'Yes Mr Grady, the client's findings and my tests confirmed that there was too much bitumous, more than I would have expected from a number 3 Mohs scale hard coal like anthracite, with some peculiar ore traces creeping in.'

'Peculiar? Ooh, dearie me, perhaps the Prince would prefer liquorice all sorts?' Puts his hand out and clicks his fingers, 'That's extra.'

Williams looks to Clancy as if to say, *May as well pay him*. Clancy takes an envelope from his breast pocket and hands it to Grady. Grady looks inside then pretends to weigh the envelope in his hand.

'Well? The muck won't walk to your Tonka toy will it?'

Outside, the gates within earshot, stands Tarrant, concealed behind a row of refuge containers. His line of vision excludes Davy's crew, but witnesses Grady's black-market operation. Tarrant hoists up his coat collar, stubs out his cigarette and leaves.

Behind the storage shed, Taffy is unaware of a rat rummaging through his pocket, having picked up the scent of the sherbet lemons. Shit! He is now. His telescope clunks against the corrugated metal shed, only a muffled tap, but enough to stop Grady wrapping up the proceedings. He holds his hand up to Clancy and Williams to stay silent and listens... He unfastens the Pit-Bull to 'go see'.

Taffy pulls out his pocket-knife, fiddle-faffs with the blade and takes a stab at the rodent. Big Hewett's canary is freaking out, flutter-flapping, attempting a cage break-out as Big Hewett snatches the rat, doesn't see it bite his numbed finger as it wriggles free.

Davy grabs the rat, slings it at the Pit-Bull, who catches it in one crunching chomp, terminating it in a mortifying squeal.

The proud Pit-Bull returns to his owner with his catch and drops it at Grady's feet. Grady kicks it away and walks on. Williams and his cohorts return to the truck, start up...high revs as they follow Grady a short distance towards a loading bay, watched by Deep Harmony.

Now's their only chance. As Grady supervises the consignment of coal sacks being loaded, Davy signals to Taffy and Big Hewett to follow him as they furtively sneak past in the shadow of night towards the Lamp Room.

****

Deep Harmony arrive at the Lamp Room to find the door padlocked below the integrated wooden shelf partition. Taffy tries to pick it with the pull-out corkscrew tool on his Swiss Army knife, fat chance. Big Hewett is not impressed,

'That's a reinforced steel Yale padlock matey, not a bottle of

Chianti.' Big Hewett retrieves two screwdrivers from his holdall so he and Davy can start unscrewing the door hinges. Taffy pockets his knife, puts his finger on the counter-top doors above the shelf divide and pushes them open with ease. An array of helmet lamps and gear greets him. He hops over the counter and smiles at the crew in the guise of a bespoke tailor,
'Just about to close gentlemen. What sort of hat is sir looking for?'

CHEESE STICKS

It's Peggy's big night, her fortnightly Tupperware Party, and the sky's the limit! All is set for it to match the *'Sell through presentation'* party plan model its all American founder, Earl Silas Tupper, developed one helluva long time before. With the tub's unique 'burping seal' – not the marine mammal, but the sound it made when the lid came off. On a coffee table with the *'Tit Bits'* magazine (like Vogue on a budget), sits Peggy's latest monthly copy of *'Tupperware Sparks'* showing mostly American women – though they could be British if you squint – enthusing around a dining-room table adorned with the titular plastic tub range.

Peggy's sideboard is just as good a display stand, backed up with her kitchen table brought through to the lounge, with Lyn's help, for the drinks and party nibbles. Herp Albert Tijuan Brass on her Pye record player kicks off the continental theme in the front lounge decor where everything matches, the blue green and brown floral geometric wallpaper design *almost* echoed in the curtains – even the poodle sits neatly. Sue, minus baby and pram, has turned up from the fish and chip shop, inspecting a plastic container, as Peggy sashays across to the musak, from the buffet table with a glass of rose wine.

'There y'go Sue.' Peggy hands her the glass and nods at Sue's tub selection,

'Good choice pet, that's a really useful size and it's one of Tupperware's most popular sets.'

'Sets?' Sue asks.

'Yes, comes as a promotional six pack.' Peggy replies as Lyn lowers the tone,

'Just a pity it's not Paul Newman's hah!' Lyn's screech is joined by Mrs Hughes who adds,

'Yes, I'd *promote* him any day' as she helps herself to a glass of wine and nibbles. Hostess Peggy steers it back on course, her toehold in *'this post-war business opportunity to empower women...'* mental mission statement gets distracted, as the acid-tongued Nell arrives, scours about and finds the pay-off as she heads for the food table and starts picking through the freebies. With as full-a-house as it's going to get, Peggy decides that now's as good a time as ever to demonstrate the product. She produces a withered carrot specimen on a plate from a box under the table, then a Tupperware container, and places them side-by-side. She then prises the lid from the container...'*pphrp*' to reveal a very fresh looking carrot. Lyn comments on the sound effect, 'That wasn't me.'

Peggy rises above the commentary, scowls at Lyn as she picks up the bright orange, crisp carrot and informs the party goers, 'Those carrots I bought three weeks ago, one I stored in the larder and this one I kept in the Tupperware.' She takes a bite of the evidence and smiles.

Lyn backs up Peggy with moral support, 'That's impressive that is. And cheese too, it keeps it fresh and it don't go mouldy and end up smelling like Taffy's socks. Kraft cheese slices I call 'em hah!' (winks and nudges Peggy).

A little later, Lyn is leaving with Sue and Mrs Hughes with their small purchases and clasping promotional brochures. Peggy is left with Nell and offers her a tray of pineapple cubes with folded Kraft cheese squares on sticks.

Nell looks repulsed, 'What d'you call them?'

'Pineapple cheese sticks,' Peggy replies.

Nell cups her ear, 'What? What's that?'

'Pineapple and cheese sticks.' Nell's not any the wiser. 'CHEESE S-T-I-CK-S!' Peggy bellows.

Nell responds as she fingers her gums, 'I know, to me roof, bleedin' nuisance, can't eat 'em with these.'

She removes her false teeth and puts them in a small Tupperware container she's ferreted out from a five-piece set. They just fit nicely.

'Lubbly job,' Nell remarks. 'Ow much?'

'Well, that one's part of a set...' Peggy says loudly with a sigh.

'I've only got the one set of teeth luv.'

Peggy gives up, 'You can 'ave it, on the house, I've got some spare samples.' Nell shudders from the kind gesture and starts to leave, but she spots a photo of Davy, on top of the TV – her lips start to curl.

'Where's 'e 'iding?'

Peggy shouts back, 'CHOIR PRACTICE! AT THE CHURCH!'

Nell tuts with disgust and exits.

****

KNOCKERS

Davy and his crew, now tooled up, head towards the Pit Head cage, leaving Grady to conclude his business and supervise the Trelewis truck load and departure down on ground level. Davy suddenly stops, which startles the crew.

'What?' Big Hewett asks.

Davy looks troubled, 'Shit, the one thing I forgot to figure man... was the cage.'

Taffy responds, 'The cage? That should have been fixed by now.'

'Maintenance would have been on that before the strike.' Big Hewett replies.

'Well, we'll soon find out?' Davy replies as they carry on walking.

'So, what's y' ma up to?' Davy asks Big Hewett.

'Have a guess? She was in the kitchen with a wooden spoon and mixing bowl when I left.'

'So, we'll be ok for a piece of cake tomorrow then?' Taffy says.

As they turn a corner the cage is visible twenty-five metres ahead with no security tape or warning signs evident.

'Looks like we're in luck boys.' Taffy starts whistling *'Run Rabbit Run'* which takes on a strange tone chorused with the shaft's breeze. It is at this precise moment that Big Hewett notices an open tool box outside of the cage and hears voices and clanking from inside! They all dive for cover in a narrow siding. A Maintenance man, Andy, mid 30s, alert and wired as a sparrow, emerges from inside the lift and listens.

'Bloody hearing things now...couldn't you hear that...that whistling?'

A 2nd Maintenance Man, his senior, Colin, late 40s, joins him and tunes into the spooky silence. Makes an exaggerated gesture of straining to hear...then throws a spanner in the tool-box. *Ker-chang!*

Andy almost jumps out of his overalls, 'Jeezuz Christ Col'!' Colin starts laughing but Andy's imagination gets the better of him,

'You've heard the stories I s'pose?'

'What stories?' Colin asks.

'Y'know...about the miners,' Andy informs him, 'the war vets who survived...who came back here, who survived the trenches... only to be buried - - '

'Knockers!' Colin interrupts.

'What?' Andy says fazed.

'Knockers! Not that sort y' dirty toe rag but the dwarfs that dwell in yonder tunnels – now those I have heard about...in fact I'm sure I took one on as an apprentice a few years back...he did all the small jobs.'

Andy prises a painful smile as they begin to pack up their tools and leave.

Deep Harmony stay low and silent as the two-man work crew pass them and disappear from view. Davy steps out and approaches the cage. He looks up through the cage trap-door at the steel cables.

'Our carriage awaits.'

Big Hewett steps inside with some anxiety, 'Reckon they've fixed it?'

'As your ma' would say, piece of cake man.' Davy replies as Taffy joins them going down in the world.

'Well, we'll soon find out.'

****

Inside the local Saint David's Church, the stirring sound of a male voice choir can be heard as two local women pass with grocery bags. A stylus rides a warped crackling record, *The Song of the Jolly Roger* as the aged trembling hand of Church Warden Jefferies adjusts the volume on a Dansette record player in an empty church.

BODY BAGS VERSUS COAL BAGS

Back at the Pit Head, Deep Harmony commit themselves to the descent and close the cage grill. Davy is about to pull the lever when a distant rumbling sound is heard and seems to be getting louder.

'What d'you reckon that is?' Davy asks.

Big Hewett answers, 'Sounds like a tub.' The low resounding noise gets louder, accompanied by voices and a dog barking.

'Shit! Grady!' Davy says as the Pit Bull terrier bounds into view and watches the crew through the metal grid as they scramble up through the lift hatch and close it. The dog growls and barks incessantly at the crew standing on top of the cage. The metal wheeled trolley, laden with coal bags, draws closer. Andy and Colin struggle with their overburdened load and manage to steer it into the rock face, causing one bag to topple off and shed coal near the cage. The Eclipse and Grady shake their heads at the comedy duo as the dog continues barking.

Grady looks at the two maintenance men, 'Might've 'elped if you'd left the cage open.'

'We did...could've sworn we did,' Colin says.

Grady shakes his head again and nods to his brother to sort it. As the Eclipse opens the cage grill, the dog leaps in and starts sniffing around and barking.

'Come 'ere!' Grady grabs the dog by his studded collar, puts him on a lead and yanks him out. The Eclipse and the two maintenance men start loading coal bags into the empty cage. Deep Harmony watch them from above as Big Hewett eases the canary cage door open and muffle-cups the bird.

The Eclipse deposits a fourth coal bag and asks the two men, 'Ow many?'

'Point-nine tons y'limit,' Colin states. To which Grady calculates, 'So, 'undredweight a bag? 12 men max.'

'Tooled with gear' the Eclipse adds as Davy above mouths *'Shit'* to his crew through gritted teeth.

'Eighteen sound about right?' Grady asks.

'For an express delivery maybe,' Andy retorts.

'We'll go with sixteen,' The Eclipse concludes and counts the bags as they carry in a dozen remaining coal sacks. The coal sacks are hauled into the cage...*thunk*...*thunk*. With every bag the cage creaks and the cables answer back with a groan.

Grady claps his hands to wrap it up, 'OK, that'll do.' Waits a beat. 'Right, when you're ready.'

Andy checks the trolley, something's missing. Grady sighs, 'Now what?'

'He left the cable remote in your truck.'

Colin protests, 'I left it?! Like you left the grill open?!'

Grady keeps it bottled, 'Remember those two bad 'Winters' we had a few years back?' The two men nod,

'Mike and Bernie? Not a patch on you two comedians.'

Grady tells the men to take the trolley back to the loading bay as they all set off. Grady's Pit-Bull has to be tugged away from his stake-out.

Moments later, Davy and Taffy check that the coast is clear. They ease themselves down and one-by-one, start to remove coal bags from the rear of the cage. It's dark, so they won't be easily noticed. They haul them around the corner in a siding where it's well hidden.

No sooner have they finished dragging the second bag when they hear voices returning. They hastily pull themselves back up to the roof of the cage to rejoin Big Hewett and his hand-cupped canary. Deep Harmony remain pillar-still and silent as Grady, his brother and the two comedians return with the dog, straining on his lead.

Colin connects the remote control box via a wire to an exterior junction box and replaces the cover plate. Grady gives him the nod... Colin hands the control to Andy, 'Now, all you have to do is press the green button.'

Andy's not amused – he pushes the green metal button.

The cage judders and starts to descend. Arthritic groans of steel high above make Grady and his entourage look up at the cables. Davy and crew plunge past them unseen, but Grady's dog spots them and goes berserk, Deep Harmony's eyes glaring back like asteroids in the night as they disappear into the dark void below.

In the cage, Davy and his crew, with fourteen coal bag passengers, gain speed, as the sound of Grady yelling at his dog fades. Hurtling downwards, the crew struggle to balance as the whole payload drops like lead-shot. Touching the high velocity rock or steel cables zipping past is not an option! Big Hewett loses his jacket shoulder padding, *zizzzzz,* which shreds like confetti by the burning 'cable-saw'.

Davy tries to open the hatch, his body gyrations force the crew nearer the hi-speed passing rock-face. *Vabumpth – krumth!* Taffy's elbow gets pummelled, he teeters and tries to regain posture and grips the cable briefly, big mistake, *zaaaaa* as the burning steel cable starts to chew-melt his glove. Taffy shakes the smoking glove from his hand and steadies himself briefly before resorting to a squat position, thus lowering his centre of gravity.

Somehow, Big Hewett's bulk provides ballast, anchoring his foothold with a controlled sway. With a steady hand, he somehow manages to get the canary back in the cage but in doing so, loses his balance, toppling the metal bird cage against the cables, creating a shower of sparks. Tweetie pie freaks out, flapping for freedom as Davy drops down into the cage, steadies himself and grabs the stop lever, yanking it back...again and again! Doing nothing.

Outside, the winch-wheels begin to strobe over a fog-distressed moon.

Whilst inside, Davy clambers over bags of anthracite, defiantly battling the express elevator to hell,

'Coal bags versus body bags – not tonight man!' Davy summons

Herculean strength and heaves a bag up through the hatch to Taffy and Big Hewett. In a mad scramble, they hump and dump the coal over the side, through the oscillating gap and get showered with debris for their trouble. Another bag – – the same – and another – it's got to be a matter of seconds before they hit rock bottom.

A fourth bag emptied fast – Taffy and Big Hewett use the empty bags like giant buffer mitts against the cables *Brrrrrr!* leaving smoke trails from the glowing glove pads. Big Hewett grabs the fifth coal bag from Davy and jettisons the contents – – *Eeieeee!!* Lumps of coal screech as they jam and grind in the gap – *Tatatatatat!* which hit the crew like air-gun pellets. *Whoosh!* Suddenly Big Hewett's brake-bag bursts into flames, fanned by the rushing gale! Hell's closer than they think...but wait...the cage is slowing down. Davy's last strength-sapping effort of one more bag is a bridge too far – Big Hewett loses his grip, the bag keels over, dancing coals around the top-deck and spewing them back through the hatch. Davy gets a pounding below deck as Taffy's coal-bag mitten whips around the cable pulley, causing the wedge of sack-cloth to burr and ignite as the cage velocity slows.

Outside, the winch-wheel spokes are no longer strobing against moon as if the giant wheel dropped down a couple of gears.

Inside the lift shaft, the cage continues to drop at less of a lick, but it's going to be a rough landing. Davy snipes a glance through the burning coal sack flames at a red marker on the rock-face, indicating ground zero, which passes in a blink.

'Brace yourselves!' *Bamm!* The cage hammers into the ground, the metal construct buckling slightly, shaking off the trauma but staying intact. A cloudburst of soot climbs the shaft...followed by metallic creaks and debris falling like a cloak, then silence, as a blizzard of black dust settles.

****

Back at the Pit Head, Colin and Andy stare through the safety grill into the shaft. Colin kneels down with the remote control in his lap and unscrews the housing to check the wiring.

'Shouldn't 'ave done that.' Both Maintenance Men shake heads slowly in synch. Grady peers over their shoulders into the void.

'Optional is it? Breaking the sodding sound barrier?' Grady asks as his brother, the Eclipse, scrutinises the cables through the grid wire and comments,

'Well, the cables held.' Colin screws the remote back together and pretends to hand it to Andy, then snatches it back distrustfully and pushes the green button briefly, then the red stop button – the cable slackness tenses and creaks. He looks across at Grady with a *'Now what?'* glance.

'Well, unless you two clowns aren't planning a high wire act, I'd suggest we haul the bugger back up.' Colin hands the remote back to Andy...who hesitates, thinking it might be a tease...then grabs it with swanky-triumph and hits the green button. The cables respond and take the strain, as they start hoisting the cage back up. Screeches echo through the shaft as everybody waits.

Moments later, the cranking sound gets louder as the cage rises into view through the safety grill and clanks to a halt. They open the safety grill and cage hatch – Grady's dog is in like sling-shot, sniffs about and snarls at a floating yellow canary feather which he nuzzles into the coal dust. Dumbfounded faces look on as eight coal-bags, scattered coal lumps, and burnt sackcloth greet them.

The Eclipse steps inside and can't figure it, 'But – – I counted 'em!'

Grady joins him, does a quick count and puts his hand on his brother's shoulder in an assuring yet cynical gesture,

'Sure you did bro'...except for the other eight that just jumped ship!'

Andy stands outside the 'haunted' cage and peers inside, joined by Colin, whose close proximity makes him jump, 'Looks like the knockers got bored with the small jobs,' Colin ponders.

Andy just stares into the cage, his ashen face patch-powdered with ambient coal dust,

'I'm telling you, this place just gives me the creeps.'

****

Two bends later along the dimly lit Roadway, a quarter mile on from the lift shaft, Deep Harmony stop, like bruised and battered war casualties at a store shed. The relief of surviving the ordeal manifests in keeping busy with the task ahead. Nobody says a word as they select pick-axes, shovels, a 'jumper' long iron rod for drilling 'shot' holes and chipping loose, overhanging rock at a safe distance.

Though unspoken, the full import of their mission and resolved commitment hits home, but Big Hewett's uneasiness is tangible. The canary unruffles her feathers and settles in the buckled bird cage, nervously attuned to the collective psyche. Big Hewett takes a moment, stops, and from his pocket, finds some cake wrapped in foil and feeds the bird.

'Come on man, let's just get there,' Davy says, with an impatience that's out of character. Big Hewett responds with an equally sour note, 'Piece of cake I recall wasn't it?' Davy rubs his knee, extracts some weed from a pouch and starts chewing to ease the pain as he speaks,

'What? Oh, so you were expecting it on a plate man?'

Taffy nurses his elbow, grimacing back a response to Davy,

'Bloody Hell, I think that pot's given you short term memory loss! That wasn't some Zen trip we all shared back there, we put our arses on the line for you!'

'For me man?!' He holds up his hand bearing the oath scar. 'Blood brothers man, together we stand or fall.'

Big Hewett holds counsel, 'Boys, boys! Listen up! Can you hear it?' Davy and Taffy stop jibing and cautiously strain to hear beyond the whistling breeze. Big Hewett spells it out,

'W-e-l-s-h g-o-l-d. That's the fever talking! That's how it starts isn't it? A tad early in the proceedings, I admit, but we all know we're trapped now, don't we?

Davy interjects, 'Trapped? We're not trapped man, we can leave any time, free will brother.'

'Ah, 'free will'...between never knowing and failure or seeing it through to the bitter end?' Big Hewett replies. He looks at his canary that has settled. 'That's some 'free will'.'

Taffy contributes with his sardonic overview, 'So, the worst that could happen is that we'll argue, which could build in to a distrust of each other and a fear of what the other might do next and a fall-out...breeding hate, then we could end up fighting, like possessed creatures until someone ends up with a pick-axe in their head. And all that – over a little gold filling.'

Davy pauses for a beat before concluding, 'Then, brothers...we'd better change our dentists.' The levity is well received – an old companion returning to join them.

Further along the Roadway, the crew's tools rest like rifles on their shoulders as they stride on. Big Hewett tries straightening twisted bars on the bird cage on route...

'Tried a mouse once, Jerry I called 'im. Course he couldn't sing if he got a whiff, not like Lulu, he just curled up and went to sleep. They used to use 'em in the war y'know – when they were digging under enemy lines.'

Taffy imagines that and comments, 'Must've been tough on their little feet?'

****

The cage begins another descent – with Grady and his Pit Bull, the former determined to get to the bottom of the shaft and the mystery – with no screw ups. This time the cage coasts, as is and was the norm with miners before the strike ensued. On the ride down, Grady dwells on the burnt shards of sacking and charred hand glove amongst the coal fragments around his feet...then, something in particular catches his eye...a yellow speck. He bends down and retrieves a tiny feather which he dusts off and studies.

He addresses his dog,

'Sid...I think this little bird's trying to tell us something', the dog barks in agreement.

Half a mile downwind, Deep Harmony approach a large alcove, the size of a double garage hewn into the rock-face to create a timber fenced-off containment stable for six colliery ponies. Their manes and tails clipped short to keep them clean, all wear blinkers and headbands, amongst them *'Robbie', 'Sultan', 'Rocket', 'Spike', 'Floyd'* and *'Emily'*. The corral of nervy pit-ponies are facing the wall and react to their presence as rats disperse from the equine feed-bags. As the crew draw closer, Davy puts his finger to his lips and signals the crew to tread gently past and not disturb the herd.

No sooner are they a few paces on when a distant dog barking injects fear into the stillness.

Davy beckons his crew to climb into the paddock, 'Christ, doesn't that arsehole ever sleep?' The crew thread their way through the agitated colliery ponies to the back of the corral. Davy picks up a handful of horse manure and starts rubbing it into his face and arms and over his sandals.

Big Hewett scoops up a palmful of horseshit with a déjà vu sigh, 'Here we go again, first y' bloody apprentice gets me in it now you.'

The canary starts to chirp. The dog's bark gets louder. Taffy glares at the canary and implores Big Hewett with a glance, 'Best tell Lulu now's not the time.' Big Hewett gently opens the canary cage door and reaches inside. 'Don't fret Lulu, we'll 'ave a song later.' Through the ponies legs, Davy catches a shadow on the rock face opposite of Grady's dog sniffing around.

The dog barks and enters the paddock. The ponies start to whinny and stir. Davy looks up and realises he has crouched under *Sunny,* who winks at him – an all-knowing *'I'm there for you brother'* look and starts pissing. Hot acrid steam clouds greet the Pit Bull as the canine bullet hits the urine mist and growls. Davy gazes up, heady with the pungent vapour and blinks in disbelief at the vision of Sunny staring back. Sunny lowers his head and whispers,

'You'll get a kick out of this' as he winks and flails his hind legs out, which slam into Grady's dog, sending him back into the Roadway, legs akimbo! The dog lets out an ear-piercing yelp, but being a die-hard gristle head, he does a U-turn and returns for more, gingerly sniffing around the front of the stalls. Another pony, *Robbie*, is planted next to Big Hewett and starts twitching, aware of the canine intruder and farting loudly. Lulu emits a peep-peep, a sweet sound as distinguishable as a piccolo at the back of the stage. Big Hewett fumbles to try and cover the bird and silence it. But his numbed hands aren't deft enough, causing Lulu to slip through his fingers and escape. Big Hewett suffers in silence as he watches his tiny feathered friend flutter away, high above the ponies and out into the Roadway...

The dog's reactions are as clinically adept to that of an assassin as it leaps and seems to float for a breath-held beat before ending Lulu's short-lived freedom mid-air. The dog shakes his head frantically – just to ensure no further flights are on the cards – as he trots up to Grady.

'What the hell you got now?!'

The crew cower, asphyxiated by the prevailing cocktail of stable stench. Big Hewett's eyes boil with rage as the dog won't release his kill and scarpers back towards the route they came and sits waiting. Grady picks up a yellow feather and mutters to himself, 'Bye bye birdie.'

Warily, he clocks the surrounds, a final inspection, and cops a whiff of the lingering odour – investigation over, for now, this case is closed.

He fans his hand by his nose, 'Phwaa! Bloody old nags.' He flicks the feather away, turns and follows his dog back.

Watching from the back stalls, the crew exhale as Big Hewett stumbles through the ponies onto the Roadway in haste to catch the floating feather before it settles on the ground. Taffy puts his arm around him,

'Perhaps a mouse next time Hew' eh?'

The searchers disappear on their quest over the roadway horizon and as they walk, Davy casually turns to Taffy, 'In all the excitement I forgot to ask, 'ow was Jeffreys?' Taffy doesn't understand so Davy embellishes the question,

'Jeffreys man, at the church? You were sorting some choir music?'

'Ah,' Taffy responds,

'He'll play some records on and off through the night like we was rehearsing – you can hear it if you're passing, so yes, most obliging he was.'

Davy nods, 'Cool man and you told 'im not to answer the door if one of our lot comes knocking?'

'No problem, if it's not our 2 - 3 - 2 knock he's staying put,' Taffy says with confidence.

Big Hewett queries what they decided, 'I thought we agreed 3 - 2 - 3 knock pattern?

'No, it was definitely 2 - 3 - 2, knock, knock, knock – knock – knock, knock, knock.' Taffy is most certain.

'No, why I remember it being 3 - 2 - 3 is that it's like the morse code equivalent of S - O - S,' Big Hewett adamantly states. Taffy's having none of it, 'Maths was never your strong point was it? If it was S - O - S, Save - Our - Souls, then it would be dot, dot, dot – dash-dash-dash – dot, dot, dot. That would be three knocks, followed by three knocks, not two – followed by a further three knocks.'

Davy's had enough, 'Hey man, when you decided on this divine code of knocks, whether it's 3 - 2 - 3 or 2 - 3 - 2 or all the 3s,

Jeffreys will kind of twig that the nutter outside using his door knocker to send a telegram message could only be us.'

Big Hewett concedes, 'You've got a point.'

As they continue their journey on foot, Taffy adds a comforting thought, 'Anyway, as he may be on duty for a few nights, on our behalf, as well as the coal, I gave him a little extra, a token of Deep Harmony's appreciation, for his services, seeing he cancelled some meeting, car club or some't.'

Davy thinks on that, 'Didn't know Jeffreys owned a car?'

Big Hewett informs them, 'He doesn't, 'cos 'e drinks too much... that's why he goes to AA meetings.'

Taffy looks concerned, 'Ah, when he said AA, I thought he meant... oh dear...'

Big Hewett and Davy stop walking and face Taffy, Big Hewett asks,

'So, what was the 'little extra token of our appreciation' you gave him?'

THE CANA PARTY

At 7.30 p.m., inside Saint David's Church hall, an unopened bottle of Bell's Finest Malt Whisky sits beside a large water jug on a Christening font hewn from granite, opposite rows of wooden pews. Next to the bottle, two empty glass tumblers have been placed. Rhod Jeffreys, of Welsh decent, and five years a widower, has found solace in established daily routines. Neither a social animal or insular, just a functioning sixty-niner, seeking no challenges, just pay-offs.

Dressed in brown corduroy trousers with turn-ups, an olive-green herring-bone woollen jacket, and military navy tie: an outfit befitting the requisite smart attire of a post-war veteran and established church warden. Rhod is no stranger to regular 'night-caps' – a comfort tipple he does not deny to his AA weekly companions, on numerous occasions when he felt his confessions somehow vindicated him. Tonight however, he's in the right place to seek a divine dispensation from the 'man' himself, with the hallowed stone walls as his confidante. As he unscrews the bottle, he starts the conversation,

'Dear Lord, I could say that this gift to the church, in a way, is a good opportunity to celebrate life, in all its glory...but...you being a know-it-all, in the nicest possible sense, would see through that wouldn't you?' He fills his glass and takes a large sip.

'You see, the way I look at things...when your son got invited to that wedding in Cana, Galilee wasn't it?' He waits a beat for a response through the ether and tops up his glass. 'Well, his mum put him up to it didn't she? Even though he thought he might not pull it off see? Well of course you do...anyway, the lad came up trumps didn't he? His mum must have been right proud, the best party trick ever! I mean, your boy turned half a dozen hefty stone jars filled with water...about the size of this font here actually.' He pats the stone exhibit for assurance.

'Well, he turned them in to wine didn't he?' He finishes the glass and refills it.

'Now, back then, a ceremonial wedding that size must have been quite a gathering, loads of relatives over and close mates...all knocking back the demon drink with...*your* seal of approval so to speak.'

He tops up his glass again, this time lacking some delicacy.

'So, how I view all that is...me, here, alone...correction...the two of us...present company much appreciated...' He raises his glass and smiles. '...is, I think, something we as drinking companions should celebrate...together, with a song.'

He fills the 2nd tumbler with whisky and points to a large crucifix above the church table in the altar.

'A hymn – to him!'

He steps gingerly across to a pedestal where a Dansette record player is plugged into the vestry PA Tannoy speakers, fixed on wall brackets above. He extracts a vinyl LP of choral music from its sleeve *'Hymns from the Valleys'* and places it on the turntable. Struggling to focus his blurred vision on the task ahead, he carefully clicks the play switch and, with a quavering hand, places the pickup arm on the revolving record.

The start of the record's loud crackling is short-lived as a male voice choir echoes through the stone hall. Jeffreys relaxes, having qualified and debated his case, absolution is surely a given? His sanguine head settles onto a colour-matching maroon kneel-cushion on the wooden pew. He holds up his glass tumbler to his omnipotent crony, 'Cheers boyo,' as his eyes start to close.

PING PONG BALLS

Back at number 79, Pitmans Row, Peggy is slouched on the settee with a Martini and smoking one of Davy's joints. On the sideboard, a muddle-mismatch of Tupperware stock, shy of just a few items sold from full sets. She gets up and leans over the buffet table and salvages a small square of Kraft cheese that has detached itself from the cocktail stick and skewers it with its partner – the pineapple cube. She picks up the Kraft Cheese competition leaflet describing several prizes: the Gold Premier Agent prize of a holiday in Spain (flying with Freddy Laker), the Silver Sales Level achievement – a seaside picnic weekend and for two runners up...a day outing in London.

She takes a bite and a puff from the joint, tops up her Martini and switches on the TV. Peggy returns to the sofa and seems transfixed by the BBC broadcast: A distinguished spokesman and Master Assayer to H.R.H., an urbane gentleman, early 40s, by the name of Reinhold. He is dressed in a navy blazer and cravat and is describing the Prince of Wales' GOLD CROWN for the Investiture Ceremony that took place at Caernarvon Castle earlier in the day. Peggy rather fancies him and almost drools over his words, which he articulates so beautifully. The sheer opulent understated lustre of the Welsh Gold coronet, the 75 white glinting diamonds set in platinum with 12 emeralds – white and green being the national colours of Wales of course, created by the eccentric designer Louis Osman... Peggy's sold. Reinhold continues his beguiling description of the preparation involved,

'The traditional coronet of George, Prince of Wales, was requisitioned by the Duke of Windsor in 1936, after his abdication and was unavailable. The older Coronet of Frederick, Prince of Wales, was also deemed unusable due to its age, so a new Prince of Wales coronet had to be made for the investiture of Prince Charles as Prince of Wales. The Coronet of Charles, Prince of Wales, was produced by a committee under Antony Armstrong-Jones, 1st Earl of Snowdon, husband of Princess Margaret, Countess of Snowdon. In the centre of the arch is a monde which is actually a gold-plated ping-pong ball'

Peggy, now slightly intoxicated, lets out a loud shriek, 'Hah! Ping pong balls!' The sheer elegance of it all takes a minor nose-dive as Reinhold continues,

'The frame was made by electroplating gold onto the inside of an epoxy resin cast in the Forest of Dean and was commissioned by us here at the Worshipful Company of Goldsmiths, Goldsmith's Hall, in the city of London. Until then, electroforming an object of that size had never been attempted anywhere in the world and it was the first crown to be made in this way'.

Moments later...Peggy, captivated by the BBC coverage, tops up her glass as the *QUEEN* invests the *PRINCE OF WALES* with the Insignia of the Principality of Wales and the Earldom of Chester...her son kneels before her. The gleaming *CORONET* is placed on his head – Peggy looks at the contrasting image, the photo on top of the TV of Davy, early 20s, standing next to their father, mid 50s, both wearing miners helmets and proud smiles, father and son championing a livelihood and family tradition of colliery work. Peggy's mind wanders, she takes a sip of Martini, pondering the privileged, the toffs and taffs, the *'Alright for some..'* an inebriate examination of her *'lot in life'* ends abruptly, as the phone rings, like a psychiatrist clicking his fingers. Her eyes, heavy with mascara and false eyelashes, blink, wider than ever, to shake off the stupor as she tears herself away from the spectacle and grabs the receiver,

'Allo? Allo? Oh, sorry Lyn, only just heard it ringing...feeling a bit worse for wear tonight...I know, I'm watching it again, beautiful isn't it? That crown – worth a few bob. I only got snatches of it earlier at the shop, the boss had a TV set up on a furniture display in the window...yeh, it brought a few customers in, I sold a sideboard!'

From her lounge, Taffy's wife, Lyn, listens on the phone against a dramatic décor backdrop of less trendy wallpaper and matching curtains – a loud pattern of large red roses battling it out with bold gold stripes.

'We're still paying for the curtains, though a nice new sideboard would be lovely,' Lyn replies.

Peggy responds, 'P'raps when Hardys has a sale after Xmas,

you can still put it on the book, otherwise you'd 'ave to pay cash if I get it 10%.'

'We'll see…or maybe next Xmas depending on things.' An anxious beat. 'There's talk that if this strike continues, there might not be a mine to come back to, the powers might just shut the colliery for good…then what'll we do? We're too old to move and who'd buy this place then with no work.' Lyn's voice is laced with an air of desperation.

'I know, it's a worry for all of us, who could afford furniture then? I know Davy didn't want to strike.'

'Nor did Taffy, but too much grief otherwise, as we all know 'round 'ere.' Lyn sighs, standing next to an ironing board with a pile of laundry, she looks at a photo on her sideboard, Taffy in a dark suit, dashing with a *Quite frankly my dear…'* wicked grin. On the TV news coverage, the Prince of Wales Investiture is underscored by the BBC Welsh Orchestra's hymn and as the choir sings, her misty-eyes become impulsive.

'We 'ad a bit of a domestic before 'e left…his tea's ruined, it's my fault, he's too proud…he left without touching it 'cos I had a go at 'im about going out – it's hard enough getting him to sing in church but…now I feel bad about it…un-Christian of me really now I think about it…it just seemed…well, a bit…*odd?'*

A lash of guilty conscience niggles…whilst, back in number 79 camp, with phone in hand, Peggy rummages through her fridge, accompanied by *Sandie Shaw's, Always Something There To Remind Me* playing on the kitchen radio, in an odd 'in house' mix with the TV's BBC choir.

'Don't worry love, I had a set-to with me brother as well – Dusty hasn't been herself since he took her for a walk.'

'Davy out with Dusty? OK Peg, you win on the odd stakes,' Lyn replies as Peggy pops her head around the door to check on Dusty in the lounge, growling at the spent spliff on the coffee table ashtray.

'I know...he never does, it's *all* a bit odd if you ask me?' Peggy responds, 'Anyway Lyn, let's surprise 'em after choir practice eh?'

She opens up her party emergency back-up supply of Tupperware tubs containing: party sausages, pineapple cheese cubes on sticks, and Ritz crackers with more cheese squares. Something rash is about to happen...

****

Deep Harmony arrive at a sign and down tools: *'WARNING: CLOSED. EXTREME CAUTION. SEAM TO BE RESEALED'.* Davy removes his helmet, adjusts his hair-net and pony-tail, scratches his head and puts his helmet back on. He hobbles back a few paces with his bad knee under the light from an overhead bulb. He takes out some tobacco to chew and unfolds Avery's map, *'DUNKIRK RETREAT – THE OUTER LIMITS Geophysical Non-Ordnance Datum'.* Taffy holds up Davy's safety-lamp over the map as their helmet-light beams chase each other over the intricate, hand-drafted relief. Davy indicates the location of Dunkirk Retreat on the layout,

'That, my blood brothers, is our coach on a cliff edge.'

Amidst the complex interlace of old seams, a *THIN, BLUE DOTTED LINE* marked *'To Fan'* traverses *DR40* on down to the map's border. Big Hewett questions the labelling, "To Fan'? How old is this map?' All light beams rest under Davy's chin for an answer, 'Just a post-war term I s'pose, *'Fan'*, *'Ventometer'*, who gives a monkey's man? Comforting to know there's ventilation down there. He's done his homework man, bless his soul, that's all that matters.' Davy taps the map.

'This is his world man, like the Jethro Tull album, *'This Was'*... we're entering a yester-year of picks, spades, and naked flames.'

They tread almost balletically as they step under the warning signs, then they see it... All their cap beams hit a *wall of rockfall,* blocking the way ahead.

'We'll have to plug it,' Davy says, 'Which means a return trip if we're going to chance blasting it.'

Big Hewett cautiously states, 'And it'll be tricky judging by the look of those props.'

Taffy inspects the prop arms, 'Them's as old as the Cutty Sark! She's still afloat though...as far as I know.'

Davy asks the military historian, 'You know man, I often wonder why they refer to ships as *'She'* when a woman on board an ocean going vessel is s'posed to be a real bummer as in *'Ship Ahoy'* major bad luck on the horizon.'

Taffy enlightens him, 'Well, in this case, the 'Cutty Sark' was named after a short nightie, worn by an attractive witch named Annie.'

Davy responds and clicks his fingers, 'You see, there you go man, they're playing with the tarot cards out in the deep blue with Davy's locker below.'

Big Hewett looks at Taffy, 'I bet that Encyclopedia Britannica salesman couldn't believe his luck when he knocked on your door a few years back.'

Davy smiles and shakes his head as he dons gloves, and from his bag, produces *explosives*. Big Hewett's eyes dart across, mouth agape at the sticks of dynamite in Davy's hands.

'Christ! Are you telling me you've been carrying those all this time? Talk about Davy's friggin' locker! In the bloody cage with Taffy and me with all the bloody fireworks going off?!'

Davy responds, 'It's cool brother, we've rarely used them, sure, but they're high explosives man. A shit load safer than low explosives.'

'Oh, is that so? Now you're the shit load high and low authority on blowing up stuff?'

Davy responds confidently, 'I'm not man, but Mr Tibbs is.' Taffy and Big Hewett look from left to right. Taffy replies, 'And...is he in that bag too? Christ Davy!'

Davy's insouciance gets a rise out of Big Hewett, 'And where exactly did you or Tibsy nick them from? 'Cos the Powder House store's got more than a chianti padlock.'

Davy takes a breath and replies,

'We missed them, Tibsy told me where to find them so I went back, they were on the top shelf in Avery's fall-out shelter where the flood-water couldn't reach.' Taffy swallows and asks,

'How long have they been there Davy boy?' Davy thinks carefully, 'Look man, there's no sell-by date on 'em and as Tibsy said, the old boy wouldn't have kept them at the bottom of his garden if they were past it, would he?'

Big Hewett replies, 'It's not *them* being past it that worries me – what if *he* just forgot they were there after all this time?' Davy dismisses that thought and assures the crew,

'Tibsy says this stuff doesn't burn at subsonic speed or deflagrate, you can drop it, you could even light a joint with them - - '

Taffy humours him, 'Not advisable, it says so on the instructions.'

Davy holds up a stick and justifies his position even more, 'Look man, he said it usually sweats when there's something to worry about.'

Big Hewett spells it out, 'It might not be sweating but I bloody well am!'

Davy's defence continues, 'Look bro,' they're a lot less sensitive than primary explosives OK?'

Big Hewett holds his hand up – he's had enough for tonight.

'Alright, I know all that. I've never felt comfortable with them, that's why I've always left it to a shot-putter like Tibsy, and not a pot-head, no offence intended. So, I don't need another lesson now on *pyrotechnics*, so spare us the lecture, please?'

Big Hewett snarls back as he produces cable and wire-cutters from his bag,

'But, to save us a trip, it's a good job I have these, isn't it? Two can play at being Guy Fawkes Mr No Sweat Smart-Arse.'

Taffy uses the 'jumper' iron pike to gouge further into a crack in the lower section of the rock, deep enough so that Davy can set a charge of dynamite – just one stick...gently does it. Davy runs a cable back and they take cover behind an outcrop of rock. Big Hewett hands Davy his wire cutters,

'And try and avoid that *'Blowing the bloody doors off?!'* scene, OK?'

Davy nods. A moment later – *BOOM!* The ground shudders with the explosion.

Outside, above ground, a patch of earth on the approach path, half a mile back from the site staff car park, heaves and subsides, settling back to a just perceivable concave dip the size of a playground roundabout.

Almost directly below, within the 'Dunkirk Retreat' seam, the dust settles from the trial blast. Deep Harmony can see that it's impacted on the surface layer of rock but has made little impression beyond that to allow them access. Taffy checks the pit-props, 'The short nightie legs are holding up boys.' Then he pats the rock pillars either side, 'This rock's untouched, I reckon they left these for support.'

Davy turns to Big Hewett as he holds up another stick of dynamite, 'Well?' Big Hewett sarcastically responds. 'What does Tibsy say?'

Taffy retrieves another stick from Davy's bag, places it in Davy's hand to form a 'V' shape and chants,

'For victory? We're going for gold!'

Davy places the dynamite sticks at full arm's length through a crevice then seals it with grit and packs it tight. He unrolls the cable to an area further back around a bend where they all duck down. Taffy's dark humour kicks in, 'P'raps I ought to say a few words...before Davy...?' Davy and Big Hewett try to fathom what in hell's name is the occasion? Then Taffy's graveyard humour dawns, 'Before we bury ourselves man?' *KABB-O-O-MM!!*

At the top of the ventilation shaft where a huge fan, the *ventometer*, is sited, colossal blades rotate, sucking in dust-clouds and particles. Just beyond this, the earth bulges from the tremor, forcing a large boulder out from the shaft wall, which skims the rotor blades – *chag-chag-chag* – to a slow spin which impacts on the crew. The way ahead is still blocked and with little ventilation and the ambient temperature rising, they begin to strip to their waists. Water starts to build around their feet, but as the dying sand-storm clears, they discover a *breach in the side wall* revealing...

A CAVERN. Davy and Taffy clamber through and down a level into a 'sump' shaft and a foot of water to find old picks, a leather sandal, and bones scattered on a raised dry level of rock. Water's pouring in, rising up to their knees. A sandal floats by. Taffy wipes his brow and watches it warily drift past the bones, Big Hewett tries to calm him,

'Those bones look canine, p'raps they had poodles back then, yapping every time they found water?'

Taffy responds, 'Well they'd be making a hell of din right now, that's all I can say!'

He looks down and sees something else in the water, a mass of matted hair? As it floats past he notices that is has a tail attached – a bloated rat. Taffy breathes a sigh.

Big Hewett turns to Davy, 'Where's this on the map?' Davy

opens the map,

'Just says *'Monastic Seam'.*' Taffy touches the ancient pit props, some are rotted, rock crumbles and falls around the collar cross beams, plop into water – it's not looking good.

Big Hewett looks at the timber joints, 'Those collar cross strut carvings I've only ever seen once...and that was in a museum.'

Taffy has a think, 'There was a mediaeval monastery at Penrhys but that's a bit far south of here. But then there's Neath Abbey, in Merthyr isn't there? Those monks were some of the earliest miners on record, but we're going back...gotta be around 1200 AD?'

Davy looks about the monastic seam in wonder and picks up one of the leather sandals, '800 years man?! You're shittin' me right?'

Big Hewett responds, 'Sorry to interrupt your archaeological dig and matching footwear discovery but right now, we're standing in a house of cards boys, and according to Avery's map...' He prods the location on the map,

'...we've got to get through *that*...' He points at the rock-face ahead,

'...and *that* is silurian sedimentary, as hard as it gets!'

Taffy taps the props again, 'We can't risk another charge.' Big Hewett agrees,

'If we do, this'll be our bloody shrine as well.'

Davy injects some positivity, 'No problem, we'll just have to dig our way through man.'

'Dig? No, I don't dig Davy, that'll take for bleedin' ever,' Big Hewett states.

'Easy bro', I don't mean with picks and shovels man.'

Davy pulls from his holdall the Damascus steel drill, and thrusts it at Big Hewett – it thunks against his chest.   Big Hewett responds,

'And pray tell me what the bloody hell is this?' Davy's monologue regarding the provenance of the drill bit is ready to roll but he can't be faffed,

'It's a...it's a long story man, let's just call it...Deep Harmony's *'Crusade'* drill. Old Man Avery had it specially forged way back when and it's still a virgin...would welcome something as hard as that man,' Davy indicates the rock-face confronting them.

Taffy comments, 'Mind where you stick that Davy boy – quite a weapon you've got there...looks like it's ready for battle too. What d'you say Hew?' Big Hewett inspects the drill bit end,

'Looks like a universal fit, if we can get a Silver Dart down 'ere with some power and a pump.' Big Hewett replies, still admiring the crow-black Damascus steel.

'Time to break out some hardware man,' Davy climbs back up from the sump, keen to go as Taffy quips, 'Well, as the monk said, 'We best not make a habit out of it'.'

****

Later that evening, outside Saint David's Church hall, a 'choir' can be heard singing at maximum distortion. In heavy drizzle, Peggy arrives with a tray of tea mugs, fancy cakes, and her Tupperware party stand-bys. It's a balancing act as she tries the door. *'Bugger.'* She knocks on the door,

'Allo?! 'ALLOOO?! Mr Jeffreys? It's Peggy – Peggy Johnson! I can't get in, the door's locked! I've some tea yer and cake for you and the choir.'

Following up from the rear, Lyn and Ma Hewett join Peggy with more food in baskets, Peggy turns to Lyn, 'It's locked, he can't hear me.' Lyn chimes in, 'Not surprised with all that racket.'

Ma Hewett sticks up for her son, 'That 'racket's my Hew.'

Although hard of hearing, the clairvoyant's perception of ethereal choral music is indelible,

'Beautiful that is, bless 'em', he always had a lovely voice did Hew', surprised he's left it 'til now to have a go...quite strange really.'

Lyn replies, 'Well, quite strange really if that's our boys, 'cos if it is, I'm Peggy Lee.'

Lyn knocks, winning the decibel level achieved tonight over Peggy, a staccato rap which seems to cause the stone arch masonry to shudder. The choir shrugs it off, continuing their rendition of the *'Jolly Roger'* ...only...it starts to hiccup, as the record needle sticks on the word *'Jolly - jolly - jolly - - '*

The three womenfolk look at each other, their brows knit with suspicion.

****

Inside the Monastic Cavern, a power cable and water hose connect to the Silver Dart drill, terminating in Avery's Damascus steel bit. Standing mid-calf in water and muck, Davy drills, whilst Taffy checks the support pit props. A sweat bath as the temperature rises with limited ventilation. Taffy glimpses his own reflection in the rippled water...his head appearing detached from his body spooks him...or was it Pennant's head? He rubs his good eye...blinks...then lifts his eye-patch for good measure. The vision vanishes as Davy has a rest, but the thought remains, which Taffy shares,

'I wonder what ol' Pennant would have made of this? Us lot...his crew, doin' a recce for gold...in a bloody coal mine? Davy leans on the Silver dart drill and ponders that,

'Maybe he's watching us now man, thinking what on earth has your hippy-shit captain got you in to.'

'Or maybe he already knows?' Big Hewett replies.

Taffy notices another floater, he gingerly prods it, catches a glimpse of *something golden...*

'Lads! Lads! I think we've found something!' *Suddenly Pennant's corroded head sculls between his legs.* It reclines backwards, ghoulish, bobbing, its *gold tooth glints!* Taffy jumps back in revulsion,

'BLOODY NORAAA!!'

Davy raises his hand, 'Ok, ok, let's all calm down, we knew it was here somewhere...we'll have to put it somewhere else as we're not here, you dig?'

Big Hewett retrieves the head from the water and sloshes across to place it on the ledge next to the bones.

Davy says a few words, 'So, let's have a minute's then resume drilling, everyone cool with that?'

Davy removes his helmet, Taffy follows but his eyes are transfixed with revulsion on Pennant's head, which Big Hewett has positioned to face them. Davy asks,

'What you doing man? It's not a bloody mantle-piece ornament is it?'

Big Hewett responds, 'It's wet...he needs to dry off, there's a breeze here.'

'Why don't you give him a quick trim too while you're at it man?'

Taffy breaks, 'That's it! I can't do this, not with Pennant watching us.'

Davy responds, 'Turn it around man! It's freaking everybody out!'

Taffy replies, 'If this carries on, Vincent Price can have my gig.'

In the monastic setting, Taffy morbidly fixates on the skull and bones, as the water drops seem to mark time like a grandfather clock, 'And if there was one thing he did hate...it was blacklegs.'

Davy protests, 'We're not blacklegs man! How can we be if we're not being paid man?! We're...uhh...prospectors man, gold miners! He'd understand that.' Taffy ponders Davy's view,

'Or maybe we've all lost our bloody heads! This whole secret pact thing we've got ourselves into is a little crazy and more than a little dangerous.' Big Hewett looks across at Davy, 'Perhaps we should call it a night and head back?'

'Back to what man? Take a good look around you, we're standing on hallowed ground and we made a pledge to each other...a blood oath...and we share a bond with Mother Earth man, just as our forefathers did and before them the Romans and before that...I can't remember...'

'It was the Iron Age before the Romans,' Taffy informs Davy, 'Right!' Davy replies, 'Cool, so...this is all we know...' he gestures towards Pennant's head

'...and this is all *he* knew and it could be the last time we set foot in here, or any other mine for that matter...the last chance to *know*.'

Big Hewett nods but dwells on the reality facing them,

'Davy...even if we got a lucky strike and we found evidence, how could we get back in again without being noticed? Tonight's high wire act was a fiasco I do not want to repeat, *Amen!* A one off that we luckily survived.'

Taffy agrees, 'He's right Davy.'

Davy responds, 'So, we got *'luckily'* once man, and...thinking about it...I've never liked working night shifts anyway.'

'Meaning?' Taffy asks.

'Meaning that...maybe it doesn't have to be in the dark hours,' Davy suggests.

'Well, breaking in in broad daylight is madder still!' Big Hewett replies.

'Oh, one 100% man, I totally agree, that'd be insane. That's why we enter legit', bold as bloody brass in broad daylight.' Davy proposes.

'What? Return 'ere as blacklegs? Then the coal Board owns our arses, we'd be payrolled, which makes you one hippy-shit Captain Crazy after all,' Big Hewett replies.

'Outright scabs we'd be!' Taffy comments but Davy defends his proposal, 'Man we'll take some heat for sure, no worse than what we face down here every day. We still shovel coal for the suits and work our stent, as close to Dunkirk Retreat as possible, but we keep a look out, watch each other's arses and take it in shifts to work the *real* payload.'

'*'Real'* has yet to be proven Davy boy,' Big Hewett states.

'*Scabs*...my mother always told me never to pick at them...but *they* do and *they* will, *Grady and his brother* 'll be the first in line and not the last to get their hands on us,' Taffy grimly states. 'So, I'll sleep on that...if that's even possible.' He yawns, 'In fact, it's time we all got some kip.' Taffy starts to pack up. Big Hewett joins him tidying away tools and agrees, 'Best idea I've heard tonight.'

Davy prowls around them, rubbing his jaw,

'You know man, the kid was actually right...he hit the nail on the head, but what he really hit was here man...' he thumps his heart '...and that hurt man, hearing the truth. He laughed in my face at the thought of another day working with a bunch of old burn outs.'

****

In the kitchen at Ferrara's Trattoria, Dino is wearing an apron and a frown, facing a china mountain of teetering dirty dishes next to a sink. A chef is preparing some garlic bread with a waitress hovering to snatch it away. The restaurant area accommodates a dozen or so square tables with red Gingham Check table cloths above which a ceiling bedecked with hanging wicker baskets of chianti bottles. The evening diners' chatter make it difficult for Dino's father to hear the news on the radio: *'Hot Autumn strikes in Italy's factories...'*

As Dino takes a greasy plate from the stack, the pile collapses, creating a crescendo of smashed crockery that drowns the radio. The shards of smashed plates dance around his and his father's feet. His Father cuffs him 'round the ear and shouts,

'Cazzo idiota! Viene fuori dal tuo stipendio, brutto maiale!' *(Bloody idiot! That's coming out of your wages you clumsy pig!)*

The rear kitchen door is left open for ventilation, where outside several cars are parked next to refuge bins. Beyond the door, a voice is heard bellowing over Ferrara's rants – the voice of Bevan, the Colliery Production Supervisor, 'Yer!'

Dino's Father walks to the door entrance. Bevan and his wife are stood outside, next to his Ford Consul car with the boot open. Mrs Bevan, late 50s, with a tight perm and maternal demeanor, is dressed in her best cherry coloured Sunday coat, clutching her handbag and smiling awkwardly. Bevan throws Ferrara a disapproving look and pulls him aside,

'It's the missus' birthday see? She's been wanting to come yer for some time...but after seeing that little display, beats me why, but here we are. Things can get ugly, what with the strike 'n all – but tonight – she deserves better than that.' Fixes him with hard gaze.

'So, how you off for some coal?'

Ferrara chews his bottom lip and sighs, 'Look, I have a business to run and - - '

Bevan interjects, 'I know, time's is 'ard but...here's two bags of the best smokeless coal you can burn at home.'

Bevan opens the boot of his car wider, where two sacks of coal fill the space. Dino appears, with a benevolent smile, almost courteously bows and shakes Mrs Bevan's hand,

'Best anthracite there ees.' He glowers at his dad who acquiesces, prises a smile and nods. Dino addresses the elderly couple,

'Here Meester Bevan...and Meesis Bevan, follow me, I've a nice corner table for you both.' He leads them to a table and lights a candle. He turns to Mrs Bevan with a congenial hand gesture,

'May I take your coat?' Mrs Bevan unbuttons her coat in a fluster, but Dino makes her feel relaxed and special, 'Allow me, theese buttons are very stiffa, it's bella wool – special tweed, quality.'

He pulls out her chair for her to be seated. Mr Bevan quietly appreciates the effort as Dino hands them both menus, 'When we're all back to normal son, you know where to find me?'

****

Back in the cavern, Taffy and Big Hewett are packed and ready to leave, Taffy responds to Davy's revelation concerning Dino's remark, 'For most teenagers that includes anybody over thirty', 'In his case, that knucklehead 'll be lucky to make it past thirty,' Big Hewett comments.

Taffy adds, 'Yes, he certainly missed his chance yer...he'd have made a good scab.'

Davy has his back to the crew. As he extracts the silver dart drill from the waste material around his feet, something catches his eye...a glint amongst the black debris. He bends to retrieve it, then his body straightens with purpose,

'Yeah man, I'd say he most *definitely* missed his chance.' Davy turns around and opens his hand slowly, revealing a *GOLD NUGGET the size of large piece of coal*. The crew stand transfixed at the glistening rock, Big Hewett respectfully takes it from Davy to feel its weight and reality. Davy feels exonerated somehow and comments,

'Well, it sure makes a change from coal.' Davy reflects,

'Maybe Pennant found it first...and left it for us man...like a baton?'

Big Hewett nods respectfully, 'Then we best not drop it 'til the finishing line 'ad we?' He looks across at Taffy,

'And you best ask that pawnbroker friend of yours to find a suit of armour for you ...'cos we're about to join the day shift.'

****

Lyn, Peggy, and Ma Hewett leg it around the back of the church to the back door, which opens. Inside the church, their squelching steps match the choir's mantra of *'Jolly-jolly-jolly'* echoing through the church hall as they approach the Dansette record player. Lyn glares at the record and clicks it off. Silence follows...except for the loud resonant snoring from behind a pew, chorused with the dripping water from their macs.

****

As Deep Harmony leave the cavern, Davy checks the map, rubs his knee, yawns, pondering the haul back. The crew, hide the drill and picks in a *manhole* – a small dark recess. Though weary, they pass the nugget around, sharing the elation as re-bonded blood brothers. Big Hewett comments, 'We leave our stuff here – Grady and a man's best friend must have used the cage?' Davy responds, 'Yeah man, what comes down must go up?' 'Only no fire-fighting this time as I'm out of mitts', Taffy replies.
Davy studies Avery's map, 'One things sure man, we can't go out

the way we came in, it's too risky if Grady's prowling around.'

'And that butcher beast of his', Big Hewett bitterly states.

'So where does that leave us?' Taffy asks.

'It leaves us with trying a new route boys', Davy replies. Taffy and Big Hewett look at the map trying to figure the alternative exit,

'What new route might that be?' Big Hewett asks.

'Our own private route man, right under their bloody noses', Davy proclaims.

'The only route I can see is back through Avery's fallout shelter', Big Hewett states.

'Diving pool more like', Taffy adds.

'After what we've found man, think of it as a wishing well. The heavy rain was easing off tonight, so the level should be down because - - '

'It's a Miocene Caenozoic layer!' Taffy and Big Hewett say in unison and continue the mockery,

'Meaning, it's close to the water table and it'll drain!' Davy claps them slowly,

'Glad you were paying attention man...I respect that.' A beat, as they know what's coming next...Davy asks them, 'So, who's for a swim?'

****

Outside the *Fallout Shelter*, the rain has given way to a mist. Old Man Avery's neighbour's son, Kevin Vaughan, aged 8, being a sci fi fanatic and avid BBC Tomorrow's World fan is still wide awake with an imagination set on full alert mode. Having never missed an episode of 'TW' or 'Dr Who', monopolising the TV most evenings, much to the annoyance of Mr Vaughan and having been totally awestruck by the televised coverage of the Apollo moon landing, tonight's bluish moon was, without a doubt, mesmerising. Seconds earlier, something outside had spooked young Kev'. A creaking noise in the neighbour's back garden, like a door opening and a sloshing sound with muted voices perhaps?

On his window ledge sits an *AIRFIX MODEL DR WHO DALEK and TARDIS time machine* – a little creative vision makes it a dead ringer for Avery's SHED. Peering through his bedroom window curtains, his eyes flick between a moon stakeout and the garden...

Coincidentally, at that precise moment, the Deep Harmony crew happen to emerge from the 'Mother Earth' ship, glistening in the blue moonlit, swirling fog, with an empty bird cage & dancing laser-lamp beams, which they extinguish on exit. The kid rubs his wide eyes...where'd they go?! Kevin shouts out to his mum, 'Mam, mam! Ma aliens mas fynna!' *(Ma! Ma! There's aliens out there!)* His dad responds,

'Er mwyn nadolig, mynd i gysgu!' *(For Christ's sake, get to sleep!)*

HIGH SPIRITS

Outside Lyn's terraced house, Taffy stops at a nearby lamp-post and searches for his front door key under the street light. Whilst checking through all his pockets, he glimpses his head's reflection in a puddle by his feet and the haunting visage of Pennant returns.

Taffy starts humming the hymn *'Rock of Ages'*, a conflation to settle his nerves and the hope that some divine ear has tuned in – as he'll need all the help he can get to explain his whereabouts to Lyn at this ungodly hour. His key is nowhere to be found, so he tidies himself up in the front window's reflection...and spooks himself yet again at the phantom staring back at him, his ghostly features and eyepatch over-lit by the cold street lamp. He suppresses an outburst, 'Christ', and resumes his choral chant as he straightens his hair and takes a deep breath before knocking...

Taffy doesn't hear the front door quietly open, and as he turns to reach for the door knocker, Lyn, in curlers, greets him, garishly lit by the dim hall-light...and she's not smiling. Taffy can't control an outburst, 'Jesus!'

'I'll give you bloody Jesus, what time d'you call this?'

Taffy attempts an Oscar performance, 'I'm so sorry love, me and the boys got a bit carried away with the singing...old Jeffreys is quite the task master, had us practicing Rock of Ages over and over again...'

Lyn goes along with the story, feigns interest, 'Quite the task master? Really?'

'Oh yes, crackin' the whip he was, *OK lads let's try that again!'* he kept saying,' Taffy explains.

'Which hymn in particular, 'The Jolly Roger'?' Lyn asks.

'No love, that's not a hymn is it? No, as I said, one in particular was 'Rock of Ages'...that takes a fair bit of practice that does.'

Taffy starts to take off his sodden jacket and breaches, 'I could do with a hot bath love, got a bit chilled to the marrow.'

'Didn't 'e have any heating on? Not even a paraffin heater?' Lyn asks.

'No pet, you'd have thought wouldn't you? That church hall and all that stone – quite damp it felt.'

'Well, I've boiled a kettle ages ago, so I'll get y' bath ready.' Taffy smiles warmly, his star performance with the interrogation is going well.

As he continues to strip down to his pants in the kitchen, Lyn starts pouring the hot kettle in to a tin bath in the front room and calls out,

'To look at him you'd think the exact opposite wouldn't you?

Not exactly action man is 'e? Hardly ever sees him on a Sunday, only when he's locking up and then he just shuffles about, hardly get a peep out of him.'

Taffy from the kitchen replies,

'Oh he's a bit of a dark horse is that one, I'll give you that but...once you get to know him there's a real...*exuberance* and passion there...the church definitely brings out his *'high spirits'*. He bites his lip, trying not to snigger, '...and I must say...that *'Rock of Ages'* gave the boys and me quite a glow...new hope in fact, for all of us,' smiles, '...much to my surprise it was something I wasn't expecting to find...but Davy and Hew' convinced me, what with the singing and those hymns...quite intoxicating really.'

'Intoxicating? So, sounds like you had a *'Jolly'* time of it then? Like the hymn?' Lyn replies.

Taffy enters the front room naked and a tad confused,

'No love, not exactly 'Jolly'...as I said, that's *not* a hymn, where's this 'Jolly' coming from?' Lyn replies, 'Last I heard it was coming from Jeffrey's record player...next to his *'high spirits'*.'

He stops in his tracks and sees on the sideboard, a mulch of party food and cake 'swimming' on a tray of rainwater,

'What's that?'

Lyn puts the empty kettle down by the tin bath, '*'That?'* Oh, that was for the choir.'

A little later in bed...

Taffy's trying hard to settle Lyn down with an 'everything's normal' cuddle...but Lyn's not buying it, Taffy elaborates,

'Look love, as I said, you must have only just missed us, we had a few drinks after and just lost all track of time. Old Jeffreys must have had one too many as well, from what you said, if you couldn't wake him? I think you're right though, he's not as *exuberant* as he makes out.'

A demonstration of Taffy's 'exuberance' is about to kick off as he attempts to snuggle up...his hand sliding down...but Lyn's having none of it, his lothario foreplay gets the brush off,

'You're up to summit' Taffy Cleaves, I can smell it and until I know exactly what, the lid stays on the honey pot.'

****

7 a.m. next morning at Davy's house, Peggy is having breakfast in their kitchen on a small formica table in a corner under a wall cupboard. She cuts her toast diagonally, creating two triangles. She takes a saucepan from the gas ring on the cooker and spoons some scrambled egg onto her plate. Davy appears in the doorway in jeans and a vest, next to the larder on the opposite side, he stretches and yawns. She checks her watch,

'I thought you'd have a lie in with the strike on?' He rubs his knee and massages his chest,

'No sis', got stuff to do.' Peggy holds up the saucepan, 'There's some scrambled egg left?'

Davy walks over and sits, 'Thanks.' She places a metal teapot and a mug on the table, adds some milk and two sugars and stirs it,

'I've got to go in a bit earlier – they're doing a stock check.'

Davy responds, 'Seeing if some dude's walked out with a settee under their coat?'

'You'd be surprised, it's the ornaments – vases and ashtrays, y'know that go walkies?' The poodle is asleep on top of Davy's dirty clothes in a laundry basket under the table.

Davy sips his tea and ponders, 'Look sis' the walkies thing and pooch...I found one of my spliffs all chewed up in the bedroom, which might explain why he's been tripping the light fantastic recently.'

'Like you were last night perhaps?' Peggy asks.

'Yeah, that's a bummer...like ships passing in the night. I fell asleep at Hew's after we'd had a few jars.'

'A few jars or joints? Funny, Lyn didn't mention that – she phoned earlier...been chatting to Ma Hewett too.'

'Did she? Yeah, well...she was fast asleep man...all that crystal gazing...takes a lot of cosmic energy sis.'

Davy takes a spliff from his jeans and lights it from the cooker gas flame, takes a deep drag.

'She also told Lyn that you're all going back? Taffy, Hew, and you – as scabs against the strike? The strike for safer working conditions so that another dozen or more lives aren't lost this month in the same mine that sent our dad to his grave!'

'You're not getting the full picture sis, there's more to it than that.'

'What more is there Davy, than *life* itself?'

'Having a *life* where there's *hope*.'

'Oh? And just how are you going to achieve that? Through flower power? Or smoking more weed perhaps?'

Davy gets up, hobbles past Peggy and grabs his satchel from the hallway, then returns and produces the *gold nugget* which he places in the centre of the kitchen table next to his tea-mug. He takes another puff from his joint and slumps back into the chair. Peggy stares at the nugget and back at her hippy brother, now he just seems pathetic,

'You know what Davy? I haven't got time for this, I've gotta get to work.'

Peggy turns to leave as Davy, in a half drowsy state, calls out,

'Whoa there lil' sis, hold on just one goddamn minute will you?! D'you know what this is man? You *cannot* tell a soul about this, not until it's safe to...d'you dig? We made a blood oath, me and the boys.'

He holds up his scarred palm and takes another hit on his joint. Peggy shakes her head at the paranoia and delusion her brother appears to have succumbed to. He asks again,

'Have you got the faintest idea what you're looking at?!'

'Sadly yes. It looks like a fool's errand Davy, even I, your bloody sister who sells settees and Tupperware to make a living, even I know you won't find gold in a bleedin' coal mine! Dad knew that!' She storms off.

'Yeah sis, you go on, don't you worry about me and m' blood brothers going back down the pit, with the safety issues 'n all! 'Cos you've got all those...those runaway settees to deal with haven't you? And mountains of Tupperware that could cave in at any moment!'

Davy's rant wakes Dusty who starts yapping, compounding his exhausting ordeal and little sleep. His eyelids start to close as he clutches the *gold nugget,* resting his head on the kitchen table... *Davy starts to dream:* Sunny's floating over the Brecon Beacon Welsh mountains, wearing a headband of dazzling gold and is joined by an umbilical cord, attached to his underbelly and the *Aur Cymru Mother Lode.* Davy's falling asleep in the saddle, clutching on to his bridal as Sunny lectures him,

'I think you could have handled that better bro'...and the grand finale? Nayeee! Putting the gold nugget on the kitchen table was a major undersell – it's just looked like something that fell out of the butter dish, you should have wrapped it in chenille at least, like the Old man did with that dirty bit of scrap iron.'

'That was Damascus steel if you must know.'

'Oh, a fancy bit of scrap iron, excuse me. Well, whatever it was, he made it look like the crown jewels.'

'Ok, I'll remember for next time.'

'There might not be a next time brother. Y' know what started all this? Taking powder puff for a walk, *man,* that's never been your gig brother, made sis suspicious. And now this scab idea? Is that to help sis and that battle-axe Lyn top the village popularity polls?! You think that's gonna work?'

'It's the only way that it will man.'

'Not with just the three of you digging, no way. You're gonna need a lookout, like *me* in the Magnificent Seven, with Steve McQueen when he shakes those shotgun cartridges like a maraca and loads both barrels as they ride into town.'

'I thought he was in a wagon with Yul Brynner?'

'And *who* was pulling that wagon? You see? I'm there with you brother!'

THE MAGNIFICENT FOUR

Later that morning, Davy, Taffy, and Big Hewett walk down a back alley, the same route that previously led them to Old Man Avery's rear garden. Only this time they turn right instead of left. As they pass a mix of fences and railings, Taffy says,

'You do know that I was only joking about the kid making a good scab.'

Big Hewett adds, 'Yeah Davy, you sure about this? You didn't exactly part best of mates.' Davy stops walking,

'Do you know what causes more deaths than anything else? The biggest killer of all?'

Taffy quips, 'Besides wacky-baccy?'

'No, I'm being serious man and I'm not talking about the mine and safety, I'm talking about other crusades and wars throughout history.'

Big Hewett turns to Taffy, 'Best let him tell us, otherwise I can feel a history lesson heading our way.'

'It's pride man, the generals and suits who send you into battle 'cos they're too proud to listen and too proud to make peace.'

'And why this particular lecture now?' Big Hewett asks.

'Because Dino's old man said we'd find him here and I'm not too proud to make peace.'

Taffy responds, 'And let's hope he's not too proud to listen.'

They arrive at a garden with a large greenhouse that is visible above the rear brick wall. *The Who's 'Anyway, Anyhow, Anywhere'* hit single blares at a distorted pitch from a transistor radio. They peer over the wall where Dino is digging the soil in a vegetable patch with a garden fork near a neat square of lawn. He picks something up from the soil and senses he's being watched...kills the volume and brandishes the fork like a bayonet in the silent after-tone...

Taffy responds, 'At ease private.'

Big Hewett asks, 'Is that an olive you've dug up?'

Dino smiles, 'No. Stones and lotsa weeds. The oleeves are in the greenhouse, itsa too cold outa here,' he indicates behind him with the fork.

'Why you all here? I'm a sorry theengs wenta bad, I said bada theengs...I didn't mean.'

'Well, you know kid, we're cool and we're moving on, putting that bad karma behind us man...and as it turns out...we're planning on doing a spot of digging ourselves,' Davy informs him.

Taffy jokes, 'And us 'burn outs' could use a good hand.' Dino looks embarrassed but asks,

'Sounds a like a beeg garden you're deeging? Where you deeging?'

Davy thumbs behind him at the Colliery wheel house, Dino looks perplexed as all that's visible is the mine.

'What garden you mean?'

'*Gaia's*, we dropped in on her once if you recall?' Davy says casually.

'You're keeding me – right?!' *No they ain't*, as Deep Harmony's faces convey.

'P'raps you gentlemen forgetta...there's a strike on, no miners are deeging any coal.'

Big Hewett replies, 'We're no miners, we're...prospectors.'

'Prospectors? *Coal* prospectors? I do not understand?'

'Who mentioned coal?'

Davy, in true Goldfinger style, tosses the *GOLD NUGGET* on to the lawn. Thud. Glint. Silence.

****

Next morning at the *pit gates*, a coach transporting blacklegs pulls into the colliery yard as the Police battle to contain an unruly body of picket line protestors. Bottles are thrown and one miner breaks through the picket line and tries to slash the front wheels with a pick but is dragged away by police.

Several miners on board the coach stand and wait anxiously

for the doors to open. Davy, Taffy and Big Hewett get up from their seats and join six other miners waiting in the aisle. They check every approach through the windows but no sign of Dino. Big Hewett comments,

'P'raps he thought it was just another stone you plonked in his garden?'

Taffy gives Davy an assuring pat on his shoulder, 'Or he's found another stone just like it?'

Davy stays silent, the pacifist scab preparing to run the gauntlet past the picket line.

The door opens and the blacklegs emerge from the coach and walk briskly through a secured barrier of arm-linked police officers. Taffy passes balding Grady and The Eclipse, who lunges forward and grabs Davy by his ponytail and yanks him back.

Suddenly, from nowhere, Dino appears like a pop-up character from a book, jump-leaps into the tussle and head butts The Eclipse, mulching his nose like soft fruit. The Eclipse collapses like an old, detonated building. Grady's looks on in disbelief. As does Davy, who gets pulled along at breakneck speed by Dino. Taffy, just in front, looks back,

'Told you he'd make a good scab!'

****

Inside Llewellyn's Fish shop, Peggy and Lyn are being stared at by a cluster of acid-tongued miners' wives outside. The usual chirpiness of the 'cuddly trifle' Mrs Hughes, greets the girls with a dour look reserved for excrement as she bustles past. Peggy takes her purchase, pays and waits for Lyn to be served. Mrs Reece enters, who Lyn ostracised in this very place less than two weeks ago – now the shoe's on the other foot. For once, Lyn is stuck for words – Mrs Reece breaks the ice with cold composure,

'Hello Mrs Cleeves, looks like there's a queue of us today, doesn't it?'

Peggy's embarrassed nod shares Lyn's guilt. The fishmonger Llewellyn looks across and greets Mrs Reece with a wry smile. He then plonks a lemon on top of the wrapped fish he's preparing for Lyn,

'There you are, you can 'ave that. He'll appreciate a nice bit of fish after today.'

Lyn scowls at her audience within and without, pays the Fishmonger and stuffs the prepared package into her basket.

'After today, he can squeeze his own bleedin' lemons. Come on Peg.'

****

Bevan accompanies Dino as he walks along the roadway approach to G40 with Davy, Taffy and Big Hewett. Bevan stops at the seam and turns to Davy,

'Right, well look after him, we'll be on tight shifts today 'cos of the numbers, so you'll 'ave your work cut out – but go easy, keep 'im on a short leash, we don't want any dramas down 'ere, OK? We've enough up top to deal with, understood?'

Davy and the crew nod. Bevan looks at Big Hewett,

'Where's Tweetie Pie?'

Big Hewett hides the tension, clenching his fist,

'Lulu took a turn for the worst.'

'Sorry to hear that, keep an eye on y' lamps then.'

Dino nods, he knows all about that and pats a shoulder bag,

'Meester Johnson give-a me oxygen mask Meester Bevan.'

Bevan does an about turn,

'Good to hear. Right then, I'll let you lot get on.'

Bevan turns and leaves them to it. Deep Harmony and Dino set off, Taffy whistling,

'Run Rabbit Run'...

The Two Maintenance Men, Colin and Andy, are doing the rounds, checking lighting and cable runs beyond DR40 seam, a hundred yards ahead of Davy and his crew. Andy is aware of a presence and hears Taffy's whistling, the same eerie mnemonic sound he heard before. He nudges Colin,

'Hear that? It's that sound again, that whistling...coming from back there, y' know...that closed off seam.'

'What, DR40? Expect it's the wind mate, must be a maze of old shafts and tunnels, bloody rabbit warren innit?'

'No, I distinctly heard a whistling sound, same tune...funny you saying 'Rabbit warren'.'

'What's funny about that?'

'Not funny really...more strange...'cos it's that old tune, from the war maybe? *Run rabbit run rabbit, run, run, run'*, I keep hearing. You must know it?'

He turns and squints at shadows behind him as the crew vanish, flitting off the roadway into DR40 like a shoal of fish. Andy's paranoia continues,

'How long's that seam been shut?'

Colin's losing his patience, 'Decades mate...gotta be at least twenty one...twenty two years?'

'DR40? What's the 'DR' bit stand for?'

'Ain't got the foggiest mate, 'Dead Rabbits maybe, forty of 'em?' Look, if you 'aven't noticed there's a strike on, which means there's about a dozen blokes down 'ere, that's two seams being worked, tops. The nearest being G40, half a mile back. So get a grip and let's get on, there's sweet F A down this neck unless you're taking skeleton crews literally.'

Colin shakes his head and moves on, joined by Andy who quickens his pace.

****

Inside the Monastic Cavern, adjoining Dunkirk Retreat 40 seam, Dino keeps watch by the boarded up entrance as a sweat bath of intensive noise can be heard from within. Davy's Silver Dart drill, with the Damascus 'crusade' bit, is proving its worth as they make good headway. Taffy and Big Hewett use picks and shovels in a fervent race against the shift whistle, inured to the lack of ventilation. Davy's gasping blue lamp flame matches their struggle to draw oxygen, Big Hewett shouts above the bedlam,

'BAD AIR!'

Davy's drill cuts dead, followed by a frantic flurry as everybody, including Dino, dons oxygen masks. The crew wait...watch the lamp-flame...as it slowly rejuvenates. Through the mask visors, their smiling eyes signal relief. Suddenly the *shift whistle blows*, Davy calls out to Dino,

'All OK out there kid?'

Dino scrambles inside and joins them. He removes his mask,

'Yes Meester Johnson, I see no one since we arrive.' He sighs,

'Perhaps I can deeg a bit of a Gaia's garden tomorrow maybe?'

'Yeah, sure thing kid and maybe tomorrow we get lucky.'

Big Hewett responds, 'And we'll be lucky if Bevan doesn't pop his head into G30 seam and wonder what the hell's going on?'

Taffy adds, 'If that happens, we're this close to being buggered I'd say.'

Davy replies, 'Not if we own it man and the sooner the better.'

****

Early next morning, in the Colliery Main Office, Davy and Big Hewett wait in the corridor. Valma is at her desk in the front office, typing a letter. She's more eye-catching than usual, with her Vidal Sassoon bob hairstyle and semi sheer turtle collar blouse. She looks up and smiles at Davy through the partition window. Big Hewett prods Davy,

'You can't afford that either mate, more high maintenance than y' usual lentils and beads bird.'

Through the window, Davy sees Tarrant signal to Valma to bring them into his adjoining office. Valma gets up from her desk – her A-line smart skirt completing the chic outfit as she saunters across and opens the door,

'You gentlemen can come in now. Nice and early before the picket rush I see?'

Davy gives Valma a cool but enticing look as they enter and go through to Tarrant's office. Tarrant's seated at a sturdy wooden table-desk and moves an ornament just so, half an inch, so that the miniature, charcoal-black cast-iron winch-wheel aligns with his pen holder. They all shake hands as Big Hewett introduces himself and Tarrant gestures them to sit as Valma enters with another chair. Behind Davy, she motions to Tarrant, *'Some tea for the assembly?'* which he dismisses with a stern look. Tarrant leans forward, elbows on the desk, and faces Davy,

'Well, we've been introduced already haven't we? Before you became a 'scab' so to speak? Quite surprised me that did, I must say, having met you.'

Big Hewett adjusts himself, looks uncomfortable as Tarrant continues,

'So, what can I do for you two gentlemen today?'

Davy comes right out with it, 'We'd like to buy the mine.'

The dry, cracked leather creaks as Tarrant sits back in his armchair, like a general estimating the opposition's game-plan.

'Correct me if I'm wrong but didn't we have this cosy chat before? As I remember, there was a small issue of twenty grand, before the keys could be handed over... *if* the mine was *up* for grabs that is.'

Big Hewett intervenes, 'We think we can raise that...between us...crew and folk.'

'Folk? You planning on getting the whole family digging as well are you?' Gestures with his head to Davy, 'Got 'im on your wacky-baccy too have you?'

Davy responds, 'Whatever man, but we come in peace, unlike many out there, we want to work and we want to make *this* work... Make a future for ourselves and our families.'

'So, you think there's a future here? That there's enough new seams left for you to work?'

Davy looks at Big Hewett, they both respond in harmony, 'Yes.'

Tarrant pauses, trying to get a measure of the mining duo sitting opposite,

'Nice to see such optimism I must say, considering the current climate, I'll give you that.'

Tarrant deliberates for a moment...touches the cast iron winch-wheel ornament then rises from his chair,

'Well, soon as you and your folk have the cash – let me know?'

Tarrant signals to Valma to see them out.

Davy and Big Hewett stand as Valma opens the door and follows them,

'Good luck boys, couldn't help overhearing...not many folk round 'ere with deep pockets.'

Davy replies, 'Just short arms.'

Valma's amused by that and pats him on the shoulder, affectionately, which Tarrant coldly observes from his vantage-point as he makes a phone call.

As they turn and leave, Davy tries to hide his warm glow as Big Hewett comments,

'Definitely not lentil and beads.'

****

Moments later, Grady enters and goes straight through to Tarrant's office. Tarrant is staring out the window into the yard where pickets have now gathered, he turns and closes the office door. Grady sits down, arrogantly without asking,

'You wanted to see me?'

'We must be paying you lot too much.'

'What you talking about?'

'Some of your boys want to give me a large sum of money... twenty grand to be precise.'

'Twenty grand?! For what?'

Tarrant opens his desk drawer and slams a *map of the mine* on the desk, he unfolds it.

'Said they'd have it soon too. Now, I know about your little scam, coal for the royals at a princely sum no doubt, but what's theirs?'

Grady looks cornered, glances out of the window at the pickets by the gates. Tarrant's map is open on the desk with a clenched fist hovering above it,

'Now, from where I'm standing I've got two liabilities on my hands...' He slams his fist on the map. '...And you! What's that hippy bastard up to? Why's he and his bloody goon show so keen to buy the mine? Sure as shit they must know it's spent?'

'I'm sure they do, at least that's what y' so called *experts* say, don't they?'

'What? You think otherwise do you? You know better than R and D and the Geo-tech' boffins?'

'I didn't say that, all I'm saying is that they know...deep down, this place will soon be mothballed and that their jobs are on the line.'

'Wrong. *My sodding job is if they succeed!* Either they're bloody-minded, bloody stupid or...bloody smart!'

'Smart? What in Hell is there to be smart about?! Twenty-grand for a coal cemetery? I'd say the smart thing to do...is take the money Tarrant.'

'Then you would say that wouldn't you? Like you've been doing, robbing the *'cemetery graves'*, as it was, for some time now?'

Grady shifts uneasily in his chair,

'Look, that happened a couple of times at most but even their techies said the last lot wasn't up to scratch, *'Peculiar'* was the term they used.'

Tarrant walks back to the window and gazes at the wheel house, "Peculiar?' I think the market for peculiar coal's had its day then, hasn't it?' He walks back to his desk and uses his hand to smooth the map out, then places the black model winch-wheel on the top half to keep it flat. He looks up at Grady with hostile intent,

'Before coal racketeering you were a *shot firer* weren't you?'

'Spit it out Tarrant', Grady replies through gritted teeth.

'I always thought that title made an explosives expert sound more like a circus act.' Tarrant places his finger firmly on the map in two places,

'I reckon you need to set a charge here...and here.'

'Are you out of y' God damn skull?! A seismic blast that scale 'll flood it.'

'You don't say? You still know your shit then? What would you use? Nitro? I've heard these new emulsion explosives are all the rage?' A tense beat.

'Need more time to consider? Eighteen months maybe for illegal trading of the Coal Board's property on the black market? Twelve's usual, for good behaviour that is.'

'So, you'll take the money first, *then* water down the goods, so to speak?'

'Well, wouldn't be smart the other way around now would it? And no casualties.'

'When exactly?'

'Well, as you've already kick-started the party let's make it a royal occasion for Prince Charlie, shut shop for a couple days, 'due diligence/safety checks' we'll say...what they've been belly-aching about for weeks and make it a sort of...belated welcome with a bang. Be no scab crews to worry about then, they'll be home with their loved ones, watching re-runs on TV no doubt, or Opportunity Knocks.'

'And what about the pit-ponies?'

'No, I reckon TV would strain their eyes.' Deadly serious.

'Look Grady, if they come up the game's up! He calms down, 'Freak explosions happen all the time.'

Grady figured that, he's not comfortable with it but knows he's on the skids.

'And my job? Where in hell does that leave me?'

'I hear Trelewis Colliery's got some teething troubles with their robot machinery – you and y' brother should call 'em' – I think blue would suit you.'

Tarrant folds up the map and as Grady goes to leave, Tarrant looks across, 'Here...you losing your hair?'

ON TAP

Outside Davy's house, in the early morning, a milkman is doing his rounds and places two glass milk bottles on his doorstep. The door opens and Peggy, dressed in a pink frilly nightie, appears and bends down to retrieve them. As she looks up she finds Valma, dressed smartly, standing there, holding a large manila envelope.

'Allo love, can I help you?'

'Yes, I'm looking for Davy Johnson.'

'Well, I'm Peggy. His sister.'

'Oh, pleased to meet you, I'm Valma...I work with Davy. I mean, not down the mine. In the office, as a secretary.'

'I's was gonna say, you'd ruin those lovely nails.' They both smile. 'So the strike doesn't affect you then? You still 'ave to go in?'

'At the mo' yes, there's always paperwork and letters to sort', Valma indicates the envelope she's holding as evidence.

Peggy looks at it curiously.

'I'll give 'im a call.'

Peggy goes in to the hallway and shouts, 'Davy! There's a Valma to see you.'

Davy appears and squeezes past Peggy and the two pints... Peggy hovers and smiles. Davy looks at his sister and raises an eyebrow,

'That's all Mrs Johnson, you can put those in my office.'

Peggy does a pretend curtsy and slips away as Davy greets Valma, who looks different - more purposeful than flirtatious. A net curtain in the opposite terraced cottage twitches, whilst the buxom Mrs B collects her doorstep milk in slow motion as she spectates. Davy steps down from the doorway to be level with Valma,

'Hey, cool to see you. I was just leaving.'

'Yes I thought you might be. Somehow I still can't figure you as a blackleg, my dad always treated them as lepers.'

'Oh, thanks for popping by and telling me but you're not gonna win me over with flattery man.' Valma smiles.

'I didn't say that I treated them like that, just me dad, we had our differences but I respected him all the same.'

'Is he still in the picture?'

'No, just me mam now. I'm looking after her since we lost m' dad...be coming on for three years now close to Xmas, had difficulty breathing...y'know, not just coal dust is it? Too hot to wear a mask he'd always say...' She dwells on that for a moment, Davy empathises,

'Pride. If it ain't us sealing our fates it's the suits man.'

'He *was* proud, you're damn right there...no doubt the opposite to you I *suspect*?'

'So you're the suspicious type? Well, you're right at home here, there's an aproned agent behind every net curtain.' He whispers in her ear, 'it's a hot bed of espionage man.'

Valma can't help bursting into a giggle. Davy knows he's on a charm roll,

'It's not funny man, I have to live here. And what makes you so certain that I'm *not* the *proud* type?'

Valma stops chuckling and summons a serious face,

'Well, as hard as I try...I can't imagine my dad taking a poodle for a stroll...even in the dark.'

'In that case man, your dad missed out, big time, on a...a canine connection with...puddles.'

''Water' sounds...more impressive I feel, if it was ever to be used in say...a chat up line?'

'Then that's one to remember. In fact, how rude of me not to have asked but...would you like a glass of water? I mean not now, with me sister here and me about to leave on m'work shift but...'

'Funny you should ask but I'm quite *fond* of a glass of water... usually at around, say 9.30 p.m.? When me mam's asleep and I can put my feet up...downstairs, on the sofa...which happens to not be directly under her bedroom so to speak.'

'Is this on certain nights? If one was invited, would it be bring a bottle?'

'Luckily, it's on tap tonight. Here, I'll write down the address.'

Valma finds a pen from her handbag, scribbles her address on the back of the manila envelope and hands it to Davy.

'9.30 it is then? Just a couple of glasses mind you, as I've an early shift tomorrow.'

'So have I.' Valma smiles as Davy asks,

'Don't you want this envelope? Feels like there's some documents inside?'

'No. That's for you...it's why I called by. It's a copy of the Nottingham contract, the co-operative you spoke about in the meeting with Tarrant.'

'You don't like him much do you?'

'Only when he's there...he looks at me like he's undressing me... often I catch him watching me.'

'Aren't you taking a bit of a risk...with this?'

'How's he to know? I've had to alter it a bit – when he wasn't around... Look, if you're serious about the mine, you're going to need the right paperwork. I've retyped the first and last pages for you and the owners to sign. You can bring it tonight if you like, for me to check through?'

'Valma...why are you doing all this? Hew', you met, thinks you're not exactly a 'beads and lentils' girl, well, that's how he put it?'

'Oh, did 'e now? Well tell 'im, he's *not exactly* right, as I'm not averse to lentils, but pearls are more to my taste.'

'I'm cool with that – another one to remember.'

'And...'why am I doing this?' To be honest, I dunno really. 'Cos you're different? Takes some guts to wear sandals here...'cos you cared for an old man.' She teases him, ''Cos you've got twenty grand?'

Davy feigns a sigh, 'Ah, I thought it was the money.'

Valma readjusts her shoulder bag, her polite smile somehow sensually charged as she leaves with a parting comment,

'Now, no playing in puddles on the way to work, not in those sandals.'

Davy calls out, 'I'll remember that too.' He looks at the envelope, feels its weight and looks back to her distant figure, now walking briskly away towards the pit.

****

After lunch, Peggy heads from work in her red mini car and for Lyn's house. Lyn greets her at the door,

'Ma Hewett's just arrived. I've put the kettle on. So, not working today?'

'Half day Wednesday.'

'Course it is, I can't think straight at the moment with all that's happening. Doin' me head in it is.'

'Don't worry Lyn, we'll get to the bottom of it.'

They enter and Peggy gives Ma Hewett a lean down hug as she's sitting on the sofa. A moment later Lyn enters with a tea tray and biscuits. She arranges her best Colclough Royale bone china cups and saucers and settles back on the sofa next to Ma Hewett. Peggy sits in the armchair facing them as Lyn asks her,

'So, what d'you think's going on with our boys? None of 'em 'ave ever gone against the union before – not in all the years we've known each other.'

Lyn puts milk in all the cups, takes the tea cosy off the black and brown flower patterned teapot and stirs the tea. Ma Hewett looks at the tea leaves swirling and says,

'I'd let that stand a little longer.' From her handbag, Peggy produces the *gold nugget* and places it on the table.

'I think this is the reason they've gone back. Davy brought it home yesterday...it seems that him and the boys have made some sort of blood oath and we're not to tell a living soul about what they've found.'

Lyn almost collapses back on the sofa, stares at the nugget from a distance then leans forward and picks it up,

'You mean they're putting us through purgatory, turning the whole village against us, for this?!'

'He's brought fool's gold home before, I remember dad letting me have a piece when I was about seven. It was...he told me it was *Aur Cymru* and that only royal princesses had real gold.'

'Seems your brother believed him doesn't it? And now he's got my Taff' and Ma Hewett's boy brainwashed like those hippy festivals where they follow some Messiah, like The Beatles with that Maharaja bloke. He'll have my Taff' playing the sitar next, you mark my words.'

'Me brother's many things but a Messiah, no. The only one following him is me picking up his dirty laundry off the floor.'

Ma Hewett puts a sugar lump in her cup and says, 'I think it's stood long enough.' Lyn starts pouring the tea through a tea strainer as Ma Hewett speaks,

'I've seen Fools gold too, it's a lot shinier than that though.' Ma Hewett picks it up and turns it slowly in the sunlight streaming through the net curtains,

'This doesn't shout at you does it? More of a whisper really. You see, it's like when you meet *real* famous people, at the top of their game, they never brag do they? They're usually quite reserved actually.'

Both Lyn and Peggy share a look that shouts, *'Well, don't stop there.'*

Ma Hewett sips her tea and stares out of the window at the sunny side of the street opposite and then starts to fall asleep.

Lyn whispers to Peggy, 'She often has a nap after her...what d'you-call-ems.'

Peggy whispers to Lyn, 'Predictions, if that was one. Surely our boys would *know* the difference, they ain't that daft.' Lyn's still not sold on that theory.

'But it's a bloody coal mine Peg', with a long history of steam coal, stretching back decades. Don't you think after all this time somebody would have found it?'

'Well, I'm not saying anything but let's just suppose by some quirk of luck they have found something. There's another thing...'

'Oh bloody hell, what else has happened?'

'I found this map in his satchel, hand drawn it was...of the mine. It explains why Davy was ranting on so much, and the charade they cooked up about the choir practice. It's best described as... something that looks like a treasure map, not like you see in films but proper like, it had name tags like *'Mother Lode'* and specific names of seams, really detailed it was, like an atlas. I searched for it this morning when he was downstairs talking to this woman from the office, but he'd obviously taken it.'

'So you think that's what they're searching for right now? Today?! Doing a foreigner on their shift? *Jesus Christ*, what if they get caught?! God almighty, if there isn't enough to worry about...it couldn't get any worse.'

Suddenly, a lump of coal smashes through the window and lands by their feet, its trajectory impeded by the net curtains. Ma Hewett wakes up as Lyn screams. Lyn dashes outside followed by Peggy and yells,

'BASTARDS!'

A hearse slowly glides past, a cortege accompanied by a funerary procession of miners. Inside the vehicle, a widow, dressed in black, stares back. Lyn bites her lip, looks back at her broken window and goes back inside with Peggy. As Lyn clears up the mess, Peggy places the coal lump next to the gold nugget, their reflections framed in the TV set facing them. Peggy addresses the gathering,

'Well ladies, we're in the front line now, there's no getting away from it, so, we'd better find out if this battle's worth fighting for.' Lyn's standing with a dustpan and brush, ready for war,

'And how are y' going to do that? We don't even know if this is real?' Lyn asks firmly.

Peggy stares at the TV set, sees the gold nugget and herself reflected.

'I know a man who does...well, not *know* him exactly but...'

The BBC broadcast with *Reinhold* replays in her head as she remembers *'The Worshipful Company...Goldsmith's Hall'*. Peggy pulls out the Kraft Cheese competition leaflet with pictures of London: the Tower of London, Houses of Parliament, red buses and Carnaby Street – one of the *Day Away Picnic* prizes. Peggy picks up the gold nugget and fixes Lyn and Ma Hewett with a resolute gaze,

'Lyn, can you phone Hardy's for me tomorrow, he's in around 8, say...I've got terrible stomach cramp...and that I've gone back to bed...he won't want to go into all that time-of-the-month stuff.'

'Why? What you planning?' Peggy holds the nugget close to her chest.

'Me and 'im 'ave got a date, we're off to London.'

****

That evening, at 9 p.m. Davy, with the manila envelope in hand, arrives at Valma's address. Unsure whether to knock, he checks his watch and waits, just by the door, checking that no neighbours are watching. He notices a puddle outside where the pavement slab has subsided a few inches and smiles as he taps his foot to make a mild splash. As he looks up he sees Valma peering at him through the front door that's slightly ajar,

'What did I tell you about playing in puddles?'

'I thought that was just on the way to work?'

'Alright, I'll let you off this time if you promise to behave.'

She ushers him in...their cheeks almost brush as she quietly closes the door behind him. Valma is wearing a large hounds tooth check cream and black mini skirt and black lace long sleeve blouse, with a gentle tug she takes his hand and leads him through the hallway into the front room. Davy embraces her as Valma whispers,

'I thought you were going to behave yourself?'

'Jeez man, I thought that was another one of those on-the-way-to-work rules?'

'Ok...I'll give you that.'

They settle onto the sofa and they kiss,

'We'll have to keep it down as me ma's only just nodded off.'

'Keeping it down right now might be a challenge Valma.'

Valma takes off her blouse as Davy kisses her neck and unbuttons his shirt...

As the evening draws on...

They have settled, post-coital and entwined on the sofa. Valma lights a cigarette and picks up the document from the nearby coffee table,

'I've heard talk of tired seams...seen reports too, from their so-called experts. Tarrant reckons it's no longer viable.'

A frisson of doubt dances across Davy's eyes,

'But he'll take the money all the same.'

'P'raps, but you've definitely set his alarm bells ringing, he's wondering what you know that he doesn't?'

'Well, that the proper parlance for a bell ringer is campanologist.'

'No Davy, I'm serious. After you and Hew' left, Grady came to see Tarrant, it was too coincidental as he rarely calls in, so Tarrant must have called him. I tried to listen in but he can see me from his office, but later I did hear raised voices...didn't make much sense but it was to do with the pit ponies and *If they come up the game's up.'*

"If they come up...the game's up?' What d'you s'pose that means?'

'Well, I couldn't make out what they were saying after that, it went quiet. All I know is that he called Grady right after you'd left because he's planning something. So...what do make of that? What are we missing 'ere?'

Davy picks up the envelope and considers everything that's brought him to this point,

'Well...I think what's missing here is...that glass of water you promised me for starters.'

POSH

Next morning at precisely 10.30 a.m., Peggy arrives by train at
Paddington Station. As she steps down from the carriage in her
trendy business outfit, a pink ribbed knit suit dress and stilettos,
a Guard's whistle blows as commuters hurriedly bustle past her
to catch the train on the parallel platform. The frenetic buzz of
the metro both excites and intimidates her as she follows her
fellow passengers to the exit gate where a Guard, mid 30s, with
Brylcreem slicked back hair and a prurient grin checks her ticket,
'Excuse me but what's the best way to get to...' Peggy checks
the address she's written down, '...Goldsmith's Hall?'
'Goldsmith's Hall eh? Haven't you got a Rolls waiting here with
y' chauffeur then?'
'No, I gave 'im the day off.'
'Alright for some innit? Well, you can't walk it in those shoes
love. You could get a taxi – cost a few bob mind you. Or your
best bet is the Central underground to Marble Arch then short

walk to the station then Central line to St Paul's then it's a 10 minute walk.'

'Blimey.'

The guard flirtatiously asks, 'Earned a day off did 'e, Parker, your driver?'

'You're a cheeky bugger aren't you?'

Peggy struts away, starts looking for signs and ends up walking towards the exit. Outside the station, she takes a breather and lights up a cigarette. Like a flamingo balanced, she checks her heel and bee-hive hair next to an underground map.

Her flexible contortions do not go unnoticed by a young mod in a Parka jacket and shrink-to-fit black Levis on a Lambretta scooter, Gary, almost twenty, the leader of a mod flotilla of scooters that have just pulled into a layby. Gary and his entourage pull up even closer, alongside Peggy, like buzzing bees around a honey pot as wolf-whistles echo from the surrounding walls.

'What you lookin' for? Love?' His mates laugh at the play on words. Peggy straightens herself and looks across at the gang, far from amused,

'Cor, what is it with this place?' Peggy's Welsh accent sounding more evident than ever amongst the collective of cockney east end Londoners.

'What d'you mean darlin'?'

'I've only just got off the soddin' train and the chap on the gate wanted to check more than my ticket I reckon.'

'You from Wales love?'

'You're a sharp one, no, I'm an actress pretending to be Welsh', she checks her watch and looks agitated.

'Well, that's a bleedin' Oscar performance darlin', wouldn't you say lads?'

His fellow mods cheer and sound their klaxon air horns, protruding from an array of mirrors and foglamps.

'Seriously, where you headed sweetheart? London's a big place. We wanna help...honest...part of our job boosting tourism, isn't it boys?'

They all nod with forced conviction, Peggy thaws, leaks a smile, Gary's making progress,

'That could be Dusty Springfield giving me the come on that could, dead ringer you are, especially in that whistle and flute you're wearing, that is the mutt's nuts that is.'

'And I should take that as a compliment should I?'

'From where I'm sitting, most definitely. Job interview is it? Or a date? Please don't tell me it's the latter?'

'For your information, it's neither.' Peggy just looks at them.

'Well don't stop there love, you've got a captive audience...we're missing a page.'

'It's a meeting, if you must know...well...he's not actually expecting me but - - '

'So, some geezer's in for a nice surprise then?'

'It's not like that. I've got to get to the Worshipful Gold Company see, it's near St. Pauls? And don't ask me where me Roller is, I've already heard that joke from the station's stand-up comic back there.'

'No, too high brow that is, you're definitely more that Lotus and leather bird in the Avengers, what's 'er name?'

'Honor Blackman!' shouts one his mod mates.

'Yeh, that's it, I can see that, can't you lads?'

They all nod with X-rated imaginations, 'Especially the leather outfit', another member calls out.

'So, you're in luck inch ya?! It just so happens that our campaign to boost tourism includes, for one day only mind you, a VIP trip to the Worshipful Gold whatever place you mentioned and...as I've got a heart of gold that needs to be valued...' his mod pals making cooing sounds, '...we can kill two birds with one stone, so to speak.'

He pats his pillion seat and gives her his best 1000 watt smile. Peggy returns the look, flutters her false eyelashes and takes the plunge,

'Oh, what the bleedin' hell.'

She climbs aboard, holding onto Gary with one arm and her bouffant hair with the other. The mod convoy of Vespa and Lambretta scooters depart, Gary leading with his patriotic union jacks emblazoned on his scooter panels, as their *day special* boost for tourists rolls out.

'For you see, so many out-of-the-way things had happened lately, that Alice had begun to think that very few things indeed were really impossible.'

Lewis Carroll, *Alice in Wonderland*

Gary and his mod troupe decide to give Peggy the 'Gold' tourist package and take the scenic route past Hyde Park, Marble Arch and Oxford Circus via Carnaby Street. Peggy's bold mascara eyes don't have time to blink as they pass through the intoxicating street of fashion boutiques. The mod brigade head south through Covent Garden and onto the Royal Opera House where a street chamber ensemble of musicians are playing to a crowd of onlookers, *Handel's 'The Arrival of the Queen of Sheeba'*. The classical rendition underscores the procession of scooters as they sound their horns adding a regal flair to Peggy's passing parade. As they head along Fleet Street Peggy looks up ahead at the dome of St. Paul's Cathedral as the bells ring out across the city. Gary turns his head and shouts,

'The bells is usually extra darlin' but I've...thrown that in, part of the package.'

As the scooter parade arrives in Foster Lane and pull in outside the Worshipful Company of Goldsmiths, a dancing troupe of *Hari Krishna* followers pass with tambourines and bells, with their hands in prayer. Peggy watches them pass as they bow to her and hand her a flower...the karma and serendipity, as if designed for her visit. Peggy dismounts and reassembles her tilting beehive whilst adjusting her pink suit skirt from belt length to decency. Gary glances up at the grand, majestic building,

'Here you go, 'Port Out, Starboard Home' as they say.'

'Never heard that expression before?'

'Course I 'ave love, *POSH*, what they used to print on the P & O tickets for them rich Brits who sailed to India, back in the day.'

'A tour and a history lesson. You made a girl from the Valleys feel special pet.' She pecks him on the cheek to raucous cheers. The scooters rev up...Gary leans over to Peggy,

'Here, I never got y' name?'

'It's Peggy.'

'Well, Peggy from the Valleys, if you ever want a tour of my place...you let me know? You can always find us down at the Streatham Locarno on Saturday night, if you're still in town?'

'I'm not too 'posh' for that then?'

'Na, not if you wear that leather outfit.'

He gives Peggy a broad grin as the scooter mods speed off with air-horns blaring. Peggy waves whilst regaining her composure as two bowler-hatted city gents pass by wincing at the cacophonous noise.

IT'S NOT GOLD

Peggy takes a deep breath and walks up the steps of the imposing, detached three storey Regency building. Made from Portland stone with its six Corinthian columns, its grandeur seems to intimidate and remind her that the establishment social order is set in stone from the get go.

A *Gold Cat* emblem greets her in the doorway of the Livery Hall reception, she almost touches it, then realises she's still holding the flower...she places it above the cat, smiles at the feline with flower and enters.

Every step of her high heels echoes on the ornate tiled floor as she approaches a desk reception counter ahead. Peggy stops and notices a wall display of historic notices, *Parliamentary Statutes proclaiming Criminal Offences in Unsurrendered Gold to the Crown*. Next to these, a wall display cabinet of exquisite antique gold artifacts, twinkling on burgundy velvet, dating back to its medieval guild heritage.

A young ex Etonian, male junior clerk, early 20s, formally dressed in a dark navy suit and yellow tie, watches her, his lofty gaze tolerating her every clacking footstep.

He walks across to Peggy and enquires,

'Can I be of assistance madam?' Peggy's eyes linger on the ominous sentence, *'Criminal Offences in Unsurrendered Gold'* as she clears her throat and responds,

'Yes love, I's hoping to see your Mr Rein*gold*.' The young clerk tries to suppress a smirk,

'Is he expecting you?'

'Not exactly, but I've travelled from Wales see and it's very important that I sees 'im.'

'Can I ask what it is concerning?'

'Well...it's a valuation I wanted to speak to him about.'

'I'm afraid we don't really deal with valuations here, is it an heirloom?'

'A what?'

'Is it a ring or something that's been left to you from an estate?'

'An estate? Hah, not really...look, is 'e 'ere? Who values all this stuff then if *you* don't?'

'I'm afraid, it's not as simple as that.'

'Are you calling me simple?'

'Of course not madam, I was merely stating that - - '

Another client, smartly dressed in a tweed jacket and cream linen trousers, enters with a briefcase and strides across to the counter, obviously familiar with the establishment and procedures. Suddenly, the Valuation Specialist, *Hugo L. Reinhold, Master Assayer*, early 40s, appears and intervenes,

'I can take it from here Alastair, if you can deal with that gentleman?'

The young clerk respectfully bows and walks across to attend to their client.

Peggy takes a step back in awe at Reinhold's presence, but her foot falters as her heel gives way, just enough to dislodge an 'awol' curl of beehive hair, which she puffs at from the corner of her mouth. Reinhold steadies her by placing his hand under her elbow, Peggy appreciates the assistance,

'Thank you...it's been a bit of a fluster getting' 'ere.'

'Have you come far?

'Merthyr Tydfil in Wales.'

'My Great Grandfather was from Carmarthenshire, near Pumsaint, yes, Merthyr Tydfil I know well, quite beautiful in parts.'

'Yes, depending on where you're standing, like most places I s'pose?'

'I'm sure you're right.' He smiles and starts to warm to her.

'I'm Peggy, Peggy Johnson, very pleased to meet you at last.'

'I'm Hugo, Master Assayer here.'

'And to the Prince's Mother, 'er Majesty. I knows...saw you on the telly I did.'

His nostrils flare with pride.

'So, what brings you all this way from Wales?'

'Well, it's a bit of a long story really...'

'Why don't you tell me about it? Please...' He gestures for Peggy to follow him...

He talks as they proceed through the lavishly appointed, almost overwhelming hall. They seem to be getting on.

'This is the third hall on the site, opened in 1835 but the Goldsmiths' Company has been here since 1339. Little is known of the first Hall but the second was erected in 1634 and restored after the Great Fire of 1666...it lasted for almost two centuries - -'

'That must've been quite a fire.'

'Sorry? No, the building lasted 200 years, not the blaze.'

'Ah...I's gonna say.'

Reinhold smiles and continues, 'Yes...where was I? So, it was eventually demolished in the late 1820s. The Hall narrowly escaped complete destruction in 1941 when a bomb exploded inside the south-west corner.'

He points and Peggy's mascara eyes follow his finger like windows of wonder,

'That was a close shave then.'

'I was fifteen at the time, helping my father with his jewellery business, it was modest and he was too good natured to ever make a fortune and eventually he lost it all, through robberies and then the Blitz. So, this is where I ended up...it had all been restored by then.'

'And your father? He's still alive I hope?'

'No, sadly, both parents and my sister perished in the Blitz. I was still at boarding school at the time.'

'I'm so sorry, that's terrible.'

'It's history now...just like this place, you can't let it destroy you, so you rebuild...make it stronger outside and in...and value every day you are given.'

Peggy dwells on that and tries to keep up with his tour as her heels click behind him,

'We've various commissions under our auspices, the most exciting one, being of course, your Prince of Wales' coronet by - - '

'Louis Osman,' Peggy adds. He's impressed by that as she tells him,

'I thought it looked beautiful on the box, bit modern for some tastes but...as my neighbour Ma Hewett said...when you see the real thing...it doesn't shout...it...whispers to you...you could tell it was expensive.'

They arrive at an ornate antique table towards the rear of the hall, behind which various wooden cabinets and drawers are positioned, creating a counter frontage to the offices behind.

Reinhold goes behind the counter, feels he may have opened up to this stranger, more than he intended.

'Right, Miss...Mrs Johnson? How can I be of help?'

'It's Miss.'

Peggy clonks down her 'Tardis' bag on the marble table top and searches...she finally finds it.

'So...'ow are you with rocks?' She produces the nugget and places it carefully on the counter, adding,

'Can you tell me what this is?'

Reinhold looks at it without touching it, an experienced gaze that gives little away but already knows...

'Yes. That's a rock alright.'

'I knows that don't I?' She playfully responds, 'But...is it gold?'

Reinhold now, a smidgen more than curious, reaches out to

pick it up.

'May I?'

'You most certainly may, Mr Rein*gold.'*

For an anxious spell he's all-business...Peggy holds her breath, watching his expert eyes analysing...then he makes a statement, 'No...it's not *gold*.' Peggy's face seems to age as she stares in disbelief at the rock and the expert,

'It's Rein-*hold*.'

Peggy breathes out and regains her youth. He looks up and smiles discretely,

'Would you like to follow me?'

Reinhold leads Peggy through to the rear small office behind the counter where he places the nugget on the leather inlaid desk and offers Peggy a seat the other side of his desk facing him.

'Please...can I call you Peggy?' She nods and clutches her handbag.

'Have a seat Peggy.' He hands her his card, a taciturn gesture that the line between cordial and business has just been crossed. From his desk drawer, he takes an eye-scope and looks at the 'rock'...his expression – like a stamp collector who's stumbled across a Penny Black. From another drawer he takes a small bottle of liquid and hesitates before his next test,

'Would you mind if I applied a few drops?'

'I thought it was eye drops for a minute.'

'Not recommended with acid. The purer the gold is, the stronger the acid is required to dissolve it. Here, measured strengths of nitric acid are used to test for 14 k and lower.'

'14 k?'

'Karats. If it's of higher purity, then I would use a mixture of one part nitric acid and three parts hydrochloric acid, called Aqua Regia, that will test for higher karat purity through the process of comparison and elimination and assess its metallurgical content.'

'I did ask didn't I?'

'And now you know.' He pauses for a beat and dryly says,

'I'll be asking questions later.'

From the drawer he produces a small, rolled up instrument case made of leather and unfolds it – several files, and what looks like dental tools, are housed in its slender pockets. He extracts a small chisel and meticulously eases a minute gold fragment from the nugget, which he places into a small white china dish. He applies a small drop of acid to the scraping and waits. He looks at his watch and then to Peggy,

'We've relied on the accuracy of fire assaying for six centuries now. Normally, a sprue from the wax casting is weighed to one part in a thousand, placed in a cupellation brick, heated by a furnace to around eleven hundred degrees centigrade – with a piece of silver in lead-foil of course.'

'Of course.' Peggy's all ears and taps her temple, 'I'm taking notes.'

'Good to hear. Then we dissolve the base-metal, pour nitric acid on the gold bead, to assess it's caratage and presto, you've got your ingot.'

'Quite a do then? Turning that into...what exactly is an ingot?'

'Well, in the case of gold it would be a brick.'

'Like in Goldfinger?'

'Precisely. Then for provenance and purity it would bear a hallmark, in this case that would be the face of a leopard.'

'I wondered what that cat was on the entrance?'

'You don't miss much do you?'

'Is that a polite way of saying I'm a nosey parker?' Now Peggy adds a flirtatious edge to the banter.

'Certainly not...but you know what they say about cats and curiosity?'

'But then...they've got nine lives, 'aven't they? So not really bothered...are they?'

'No...good point Miss...Peggy. So, going back to the gold brick... the 'Goldfinger' bar, the term 'Hallmark' derives from these premises, so the gold brick would have our official Goldsmith's Hall mark, the leopard.'

He moves the china dish aside and looks at the clock above the door.

'So, we'll soon have an answer for you.'

Peggy looks dismayed and agitated.

'Ow soon?'

'Are you around next week?'

'Next week?! Only if I win the Kraft competition.'

'Craft? As in the arts?'

'No. Cheese, as in the sandwiches. Any chance of sooner?'

Screw the social divide, these people like each other. Reinhold playfully mimics her accent,

'Ow soon?' Peggy's demurring smile and fluttering eyelashes win the day as Reinhold refits his eye glass scope and finds a small pen torch which he shines at the nugget.

'Well...let's have a closer look...let me see...'

The gold undulating surface makes the light beam coruscate and shimmer. Reinhold's gaze seems transfixed in a frozen moment...he switches off the torch and removes his eye mono-scope.

'It's gold alright, no question about it, possibly the finest sample – in terms of its size and purity that is – of raw Welsh Gold I've ever encountered. Welsh gold, as you may know, due to its scarcity and origins, is highly sought after and prized by the Royal - - '

Peggy becomes impatient, 'Yes – but what's it worth?'

'There was a chalice of similar caratage to this that was auctioned at Christies I believe, for seven hundred and ten pounds...' Peggy looks crest-fallen but Reinhold hasn't finished,

'...back in 1892.'

'1892 you say?' Peggy purses her lips and makes a soft breeze-whistle.

'Yes. How did you come to - - ?'

'Uh...mother, left it...in an old pocket.'

'Not an old seam perhaps?' Peggy knows he suspects,

'Old seam?'

'Often we find things that fall through holes don't we? And end up in...seams?'

Peggy looks at Reinhold with an earnest urgency,

'It would be a timely thing if it was valuable...we've had a tough time of it back home, with the miners' strike and a lot of coal mines shutting...'

'Yes, I've read about it, must be a very challenging time for the mining community?'

'Me dad always thought 'e had a job for life, like most families... it's all we've known for decades, and...now, just me and me brother...we just don't know what's in store any more, this year or next.'

'Is he a miner?'

Peggy nods, tries to hold back a tear but sits upright and dignified. Reinhold picks up the nugget and leans forward as if confiding with Peggy,

'Well, it's a pity *your mother* doesn't have any more? As far as we're concerned, its value in its raw unannealed state is only four and a half to five - - '

'Pounds?'

'Oh pounds, Peggy, most certainly.' A beat as he considers his assessment,

'Yes...I'd say that's about right...four and a half to five *thousand pounds*, is only an estimate mind you.'

Holy shit! Peggy plays it cool, as Agent Tupperware kicks in... she notices a stale sandwich on a plate on Reinhold's desk. From her handbag she retrieves a Tupperware sandwich tub and points to the plate.

'You should 'ave a proper container for that?'

'I should 'ave a proper lunch too more like.' He carefully considers what he says next.

'There's a nice place around the corner and...look, forgive my presumptuousness...'

'I would...if I could say it.'

'Well, what I was going to suggest is, if you like, we can walk through the gardens here on the way and you could enlighten me about *'Mother'*?

'Well, I s'pose...I am a bit peckish after the palaver of getting here, especially the ride.'

'Ride? Did you not come by train?'

'Oh yes, I did that...then I took a scooter.'

'You took a scooter on the train?'

'No, silly, there was one waiting. You can get everything in London can't you? Not like back 'ome.'

Reinhold, totally captivated by this Welsh lass from the Valleys, finds a Royal blue, velvet pouch bearing the gold embossed leopard hallmark. He slips the gold nugget inside and hands it back to Peggy. As they set off, Peggy feels relaxed like you do in company you instinctively trust, as Reinhold engages her in conversation.

****

Later at Simpson's Tavern, a waiter brings Reinhold and Peggy two coffees and leaves,

'I've never 'ad a waiter bring me coffee in a pub before.'

'This Tavern's been here for over 200 years.'

'Well it was lovely, thank you...s'pose you won't need the

Tupperware now, but you can 'ave that on me.'

Peggy checks her watch, tries to hide her anxiety, Reinhold places his hand on her arm,

'Don't worry, we'll get a cab to the station...unless you've booked your scooter friend?'

'No, I've had that tour...I'm back at work tomorrow so best get home.'

'So...about *'Mother'?*'

'Ah, well, I expect my brother Davy would best describe her as... being very *deep* I s'pose.'

'Yes, I can see that might be the case.'

'Also...*Mother'* may have a *'lode'* of stuff that he's looking at right now, if you get my drift?'

'Then, that's a more serious matter Peggy, that would require... shall we say an unorthodox approach to the established protocol, and one I *may* be able to assist you with? However, it's all contingent on ownership rights because if the coal board shuts the mine, it will still remain under their jurisdiction being their acquisition. Is this being addressed by your brother and obviously the crew involved?'

Peggy looks flustered,

'I don't know...I haven't thought that far ahead...didn't really think it would get to this stage...didn't really think this could happen.'

The waiter appears with the bill and Reinhold looks up,

'Just put it on the tab George.'

'Certainly Mr Reinhold.' Reinhold signs the chit and the waiter leaves.

'Look Peggy, with the current mine closures the coal board may be only too pleased to get it off their hands. If that's the case then two things need to happen, firstly, your brother needs to find that Mother Lode...because if he does, the second thing that will need to happen is...you'd better have those legal papers signed.'

'HE HAS HELD THIS'

Back at number 79 Pitman's Row, Peggy holds court in her lounge with a gathering of folk who know of Davy's discovery. Shoe-horned into the room, seated on the settee, lounge recliner and kitchen table chairs, are Davy, Valma, Taffy, Lyn, Big Hewett, Ma, and Dino.

On the sideboard sits a Tupperware reserve buffet selection of nibbles. Dino tries a pineapple cheese stick whilst stroking the poodle and looks at Peggy with mild discomfort as Davy watches him, remembering the *'Sillier hairdo'* comment. Peggy 'chairs' the meeting and kicks off by tapping a spoon on a Babycham glass,

'Right, there's some food on the table so please help yourself. Firstly, thank you all for coming. We all know why we're here and that I've been up to London and had the nugget that you boys found valued, with a bloke I trust and one I think could help us.'

All eyes focus on the coffee table where the glittering golden nugget is sitting on top of the Royal blue velvet pouch with its gold embossed leopard emblem.

Davy interrupts, 'I bet he could man.'

Peggy comes clean, 'Look...I'll be honest...I was proper flabbergasted when Hugo told me what it's worth - - '

'Ooh, Hugo is it? And who's he when 'es at home sis?'

Peggy clears her throat, 'Hugo Reinhold is the Worshipful Gold Company's Master Assayer to the Queen.'

Davy looks at Valma as everybody sits open-jawed.

'You what? Your *bloke* knows the *Queen*? Holy shit sis', you 'ave been hob-nobbing it big time. How in the world did you get in touch with 'im?'

Peggy subconsciously switches to a slightly more articulate voice,

'I saw him on TV...he was talking about the Prince of Wales' crown...it was quite fascinating actually...the company he works for commissioned it.'

Davy responds, 'Well, well...talk about connected.'

Lyn throws caution into the proceedings,

'But can you trust 'im Peg? You've only just met this man and suddenly you're rubbing shoulders with y' betters in the big city, it's a different league pet?'

'He is not my *'Betters'* or yours or anybody else's and does not pretend to be, there's no airs and graces about him. His Great Grandfather came from Carmarthenshire...I think he said Pumsaint...he could have taken me to a posh restaurant to impress me but he didn't, we ended up in a pub chatting over a coffee...well tavern actually.'

Davy leans forward, 'He took you to dinner? Coffee in a tavern? And that ain't posh man?'

'In fact, d'you know where the term 'POSH' comes from? It means 'Port Out, Starboard Home' from when the upper crust travelled to India.'

Lyn asks suspiciously, 'And this toffee nose told you that I suppose and he's not posh?'

'No, a young mod on a scooter did, if you must know, Gary, who gave me a lift to his place, not *his* place, though he'd 'ave liked to, but Goldsmith's Hall.'

It all goes quiet as all assembled try to connect with their visual image of Peggy's curious day.

'Another thing he said, not the mod but Hugo, over dinner, he said that if we're gonna pull this off, before we start buying new... sideboards or holidays or houses, *we need to buy the mine.*'

Davy responds, 'Well lil' sis, though we 'aven't been moving in your grand circles, with coffees in pubs that aren't pubs, we have been doing some cool moves ourselves.' He nods to Valma who produces the legal document and speaks to all gathered,

'OK...I'm Valma by the way, I uh...work at the colliery in the office, though for how long with all that's happening, who knows? Anyway, I drafted this legal document a couple of days ago, it's based on a similar one where miners up north bought their mine as a co-operative. It'll need signatures from those of you who plan to be shareholders.'

'And what's in it for you love?' Lyn asks.

'Same as what's in it for all of us...a future, I hope?' Valma replies, endorsed by Davy who puts his arm around her and smiles.

'Ow' much ees thees a mine gonna cost?' Dino asks.

'A cool twenty grand is what Tarrant proposed,' Davy informs the group. Dino blows a muted whistle through his lips in astonishment.

'Twenty grand!' Peggy exclaims. 'You never mentioned that!'

'You never asked.'

'How are we going to raise that sum? And what if that nugget's all there is?' Lyn, the ever sceptic asks.

'Then it's the shareholders who put their money where their mouth is and take that risk.' Peggy replies as she grabs her handbag and throws a wad of money on the coffee table,

'There's three grand there for starters, two of which is from our ma's place.' She looks across at Davy, who is deeply touched and nods a thank you for believing in him,

'Nobody must tell a soul outside of this circle...are we all cool with that?' Davy asks. Everybody nods and agrees.

Peggy scribbles something in a small notebook, adding,

'I'll make a note of who puts in what for how many shares.'

Big Hewett looks at Peggy, 'I'll match that, I've some Post Office savings, I think it takes a few days to draw it out but I'm in.'

Taffy looks at Lyn for approval, Lyn responds,

'Well, the bleedin' sideboard 'll 'ave to wait. We're in, so put that in your book.' Taffy gives Lyn a peck on the cheek and a cuddle, Lyn playfully extracts herself from the embrace as Taffy makes a statement,

'So, in reality, we're eleven grand light? What if the shortfall is a bridge too far for us?'

Peggy responds, 'I can sort some more Tupperware parties, Reg' at the Co-op said he'd take some.'

Lyn adds, 'I'll help you pet and...maybe we can organise a street party for...the Prince of Wales?! We can have a few stalls and sell cakes and some old clothes?'

Dino stands up, 'I would aska my old man to 'elp with food but he is *avaro*, mean with *denaro* and he talka too much, would tell many souls...but I ava some money saved so, I'm gooda for five 'undred pounds.'

Davy lights up a joint, 'Nice one kid, now we're cookin', we're gonna get there man.'

Valma says, 'I can do the same as Dino, you can put me down for £500, I can get it tomorrow.'

Davy kisses Valma passionately on the lips. Mild excitement builds as individuals pledge funds, Dino sits down as Taffy stands up,

'Ok, looks like we're half-way there. Peggy? Your London gent... you said his Great Grandfather came from Pumsaint didn't you?'

'That's what he told me, yes,' Peggy replies.

'Does that ring any bells here?' Taffy asks. Everybody looks non-plussed, Taffy rubs under his eye patch then straightens it and enlightens them,

'Well, it may be a coincidence but...it's part of the estate of Dolaucothi, it means the *Five Saints, Mwynfeydd Aur* where they mined gold in Roman times and I hear some locals worked it on a small scale before the war. Your gentleman would know that Peggy.

Now, I'm not implying any ulterior motive here, as I believe your Mr Reinhold would share our Welsh roots and values, so...I feel that we might have a common interest here surely?'

Ma Hewett, who's remained silent up until now, picks up the gold nugget, cradling it with both hands...as she connects and tunes into its vibrations...

'He has held this...your gentleman...a lonely figure, an orphan perhaps? He knows its value and our crusade to seize the dragon's tail...I think you've found yourself one of those saints.'

****

Deep Harmony are all tooled up with 'mandrill' picks and hardware and lead 'Sunny' the Pit Pony, laden with gear over the roadway horizon. The crew pass a handful of other 'Blacklegs' and dock their helmets in unity on route to their seams as Dino smiles but hangs back to watch them pass, ensuring they are out of view when he and the 'Burn outs' head towards DR40. As the other crew disappear into the distance, Taffy and Davy start singing as Dino catches up and signals *'All clear'*.

Deep Harmony split up. Davy, Sunny, and Dino head for DR40 – the young blood will earn his cut whilst Taffy and Big Hewett leg it to the legit G40 seam to address any early inspection visit from Bevan.

At the DR40 seam, Davy reacquaints Dino with the Silver Dart drill operation and reconfiguration with the 'crusade' drill bit.

'OK, soldier, this is one battle we're gonna win – armed with this.'

'What ees so special about that?'

'Our secret weapon man, this is your combat drill, it's meaner, faster, and it's gonna get a lot hotter in there so keep the water pressure on – we don't want you or that drill bit having a meltdown.'

Dino nods and starts to drill, shouting out triumphantly,

'Qui verso mio vecchio e lavoro in cucina!' *(Here's to my old man and kitchen work!)*

Davy massages his knee and chews some wacky-baccy to relieve the bone deep ache as he clambers out to the entrance to keep a look out and check on Sunny. The pit pony lowers his head and looks over his blinkers at the kid, then back to Davy and comments,

'Has he upset you again?'

'No, man, he's just blowing off a bit of steam that's all.'

'And you've deduced that from your masterful command of Italian I presume?'

'You can presume all you like but we're cool OK?'

'Then why are you out here?'

Davy strains to look beyond Sunny in all directions, 'Just keeping an eye out man.'

'No need to, I'm here for you brother, I'm your neighbourhood watch, your eyes and ears, your command post sentry, your - - '

'Alright, I get it! Just...let me know if you see anything OK man?'
'Shall I winnie? Or maybe a loud neigh or snort? What if I stamp my hoof defiantly like those stallions do in the movies before they take off or...?'

Davy pats Sunny and shakes his head to dislodge the imaginary discourse, as he returns to assist Dino.

An hour later, Taffy and Big Hewett join them as they all take turns to drill. As one takes over 'sentry duty' at the entrance, the other three drill and hack in a frantic race against the clock. They use mandrill picks, the debris falling away into a foot of water and a stifling swamp of air dust.

As the crew edge further and further in, the time consuming process of securing arm and collar props eats into their shift time. The 'burn outs' begin to tire. As for gold nuggets or a glint of hope? Still no sign. Davy produces a stick of dynamite from his rucksack,

'We'll go easy man, just a wake up call for mother.'

'And let's pray nobody else?' Big Hewett replies as he does a final inspection of the pit props.

Taffy sets a charge. Davy does a final check outside, pats Sunny on the head then returns to haul Dino back as the crew scramble for cover.

Davy shouts out, 'Heads down!'

Boom! The ground quakes. Rocks crash into the water leaving a dust-swill hanging in the air. Davy strains to read his lamp flame. Dino checks it – thumbs up – normal.

Above them, at the top of the ventilation shaft where the main fan rotates, a huge boulder shifts further out. It brushes the fan's outer rim like an oversized flint-wheel – *za-za-za-za*. The rotary blades slow to a merry-go-round.

Outside by the pit gates – shockwave ringlets form in 'Dusty's puddle', unnoticed by The Eclipse and the pickets...the water drains away through a hairline fissure.

Meanwhile, inside the cavern, a coal dust-cloud hangs. Pit-props creak as the roof sheds debris. But the 'House of cards' they're in seems to be holding up.

Davy gives a signal to Dino to resume drilling, a procedure now ingrained in the kid as he triggers the water hose, followed by the drill. Visibility is down to a metre, enough to see the black pool of water that has now risen to mid-calf level.

A distant shift whistle blows. The crew down tools. Frustrated, they feel their way out. Davy's tender knee joint causes him to tread carefully and adopt a limp requiring Big Hewett to assist as they cautiously emerge onto the roadway. Davy clambers onto Sunny's back to relieve the pressure on his knee joint and pats him, feels that his ribs are prominent, as he forages Davy's hand for food,

'Who's feeding the ponies man?'

Big Hewett replies, 'Can't say I've seen a Haulier today.'

'What if they're on strike?' Davy asks like an overly concerned inebriate wrestling with overdue concern whilst fathoming a plan of action.

Davy chews hard on some wacky-baccy, woozily fights the chronic ache, leans forward and hugs Sunny like a long lost friend,

'Don't you worry man, *my turn* to look-out for *you* now brother.'

Davy assures Sunny with several hardy pats as he shakes a pretend shotgun cartridge a la Steve McQueen style and delivers the line,

'I'll be riding shotgun man.'

The crew shoot Davy a look reserved for mental defectives as Deep Harmony head for home.

****

The village enterprise to raise the shortfall of funds gets underway, with Peggy and Lyn masterminding the operation on several fronts. Plan 'A' kicks off with Ma Hewett spearheading the proceedings with a biscuit tin, one of a number of different sized and shaped biscuit tins she's collected over the decades, Huntley and Palmers, Jacob's, Carr Company, the Coronation Luxury Biscuit, Crawfords and the CWS Co-operative Society biscuit selection, all suitably proportioned to store Ma Hewett's cake bakery production output.

However, one particular receptacle escaped Ma's larder, a Peek Frean's Playbox assorted biscuit tin. Its destination was decided one afternoon, many years ago, with Mrs Jeffries, the belated church warden's wife. They sipped tea...and after the last biscuit was dunked and consumed, the tea leaves were ritualistically read. A burglary was predicted, with money being stolen from within the household...and the golden emptiness of the Peek Frean tin glowed amongst the scattered crumbs. It caught the garden sunlight in a blinding glare, sealing its fate as the chosen one – the only biscuit tin to be buried beyond the rhubarb, under the runner bean patch, behind the glass potting shed. The only biscuit tin containing Ma Hewett's savings...two hundred and forty three pounds and ten shillings.

****

Next up is Lyn, who hits the ground running with Plan 'B', in her Pilgrim chisel-toed mid platform shoes with two suitcases containing an old fur coat, a wedding dress, a Coronation tea set and some of Taffy's uniforms. At the pawn shop, in the store room, at the rear, a boiling kettle whistles...Stan, the owner, is making tea and watching a BBC News item on TV, showing excerpts from the Woodstock music festival. It switches from The Who to the sweat-drenched black folk singer Richie Havens singing, *'It's a long hard road'*. The shop door bell tinkles, as the door that often sticks, judders...Stan pops his head out from the store room and sees Lyn laden with luggage.

'Hello Lyn, off anywhere nice?'

'No, stuck in this dump with you Stan, so best put the kettle on.'

'Well, you're in luck, it's just boiled...either that or somebody saw you coming and gave you a wolf-whistle.' Lyn gives him a withering look, Stan resumes the repartee,

'So, let me guess? Either you've finally decided to leave him or it's part of that two point six million from the Great Train Robbery you want me to launder?'

'Blimey, you must 'ave X Ray eyes...but what's in the second bag?'

'Ah, you've got me there.'

'Then best I show you.'

Stan helps Lyn place the 2nd suitcase on the counter and helps her unfasten the catches. Lyn pulls out one of Taffy's regimental tunics and gives it a shake to un-crease it. A button flies off and pings the glass counter.

'Now, he's only worn this once.' Stan picks up the brass button and inspects the tatty garment,

'And which battle was that?'

****

Outside the local Co-operative Store, a delivery van is backing up into a tight space outside the entrance, watched by Reg', the shopkeeper, just as Peggy nips in with her red Mini and parks. Reg' calls out and thumps the van hard to halt, as the van driver slams on the brakes, leaving the vehicle stranded, half in, half out into the street. Reg' strides a couple of paces to the red Mini and shouts at the driver,

'Oi! You can't park there!'

Peggy checks her hair in the mirror and applies some more lipstick, whilst Reg' is seeing red and trying to identify the cheeky bastard at the wheel,

'Did you hear me? I've got a delivery here!'

Peggy hops out of her Mini with her all business demeanour and opens the passenger door to retrieve one of 3 large boxes,

'Oh, it's you.' Reg's face assumes its usual default grimace.

'I know you have Reg'. Mine. Three boxes – where d'you want them?'

She pulls out a rose pink sample, every bit as vibrant as her pink lipstick and matching, complimentary smile, just like the American wives do in the Tupperware brochure. The van driver toots his horn impatiently as Reg's gaze fixes on the pink, then the other two boxes on the car seat and back to Peggy,

'I don't suppose you do them in – ?'

'No luv', just the pink.'

****

It's midday and the Pitmans Row street party gets underway with the weather due to, hopefully, brighten up, according to Ma Hewett's inclement morning forecast, which might have been a little more detailed if the postman hadn't called mid trance with a parcel delivery. However, looking on the bright side, Ma Hewitt's kitchen was in overdrive the night before, which a mountain of Bara brith cakes, sultana scones and three Victoria sponges sitting on a table outside attests to.

Neighbouring next to Ma's baking bonanza, we find Lyn's stall – consisting of a folding decorator's wall-papering table, upon which a suitcase worth of stuff Stan at the pawn shop had passed on.

Peggy returns from the Co-op and parks her Mini outside number 79, narrowly missing a boy who bounces into view on a space hopper and is hauled back by his mum. Peggy smiles as she looks through her windscreen, feels a real sense of accomplishment as she sees all the banners and bunting straddling the street. Several families gather with their children as Lyn greets Peggy and helps her set up her Tupperware stall. A dozen or so tables are joined end to end at the far end of the street, forming a long display of sandwiches, party snacks, and lemonade which Mrs B is supervising with a central tea urn and biscuits under a union jack and Welsh flag banner.

A small number of people gather, waiting their turn to have their fortunes told by Ma Hewett's tea leaf readings. At the opposite end of the table sit the raffle prizes, a metal gold plated spinning ashtray and a Tretchikoff Tina Nymph painting of a Spanish women, courtesy of Peggy's furniture store. Alongside, a rose patterned tin of Co-op biscuits Reg the manager donated for the community celebration. Lyn picks up the tin, admiring the ornate rose still-life painting on the lid and turns to Peggy,

'Did you 'ave to buy those?'

'No, I think Reg' felt a bit guilty not taking all three boxes off me, so he donated them to the cause.'

They both look at the families and locals now filling the street, and feel awkward about the real motivation behind it all...Lyn confides in Peggy,

'You know Peg', if we pull this off, we'll 'ave saved a coal mine and all these families. It'll all work out pet.'

Peggy mulls the thought and nods...watching a cloud's shadow move across the stalls as if some divine dust-sheet had been slowly pulled from beyond the valley, allowing light to descend. Peggy looks down the street at the bustling activity and then something gold, a vehicle, moving in the distance, draws closer and comes into view...her rapt attention now focused on a Rolls Royce Silver Shadow that is slowly approaching.

Residents study the distinguished visitor as he walks into the decorated party section, dressed in a hounds tooth sports jacket, powder blue shirt and cravat and cream trousers. Heads turn in fascination and observe his every move as he approaches the table and his gaze meets Peggy's.

'I parked outside of your house, hope that's alright?'

'Well, I might have to have a word with the warden.'

The silence that follows is laced with reserved excitement.

'Any chance of a cup of tea and a piece of cake while you check?'

'Certainly Mr Reinhold...I have your table reserved...shall I put it on your tab?'

Reinhold smiles and hands over a five pound note as Peggy sorts it with Mrs B and returns with a mug of tea and selection of cakes on a plate.

Within arm's reach, or rather ear-reach, a curious housewife picks up one of Peggy's Tupperware containers from her display table and examines it, Reinhold leans across and confides to the woman,

'That would be a wise investment, my lunch breaks have never been the same since.'

The housewife smiles at them both and pays Peggy. Approaching...from the east-side, Lyn checks her reflection in her front room window, tidies her hair, and brush-pats the creases from her dress before sauntering over.

'Well Peggy, aren't you going to introduce us?'

Peggy responds, 'Lyn, this is Mr Reinhold...Hugo Reinhold, from the Worshipful Company, he's travelled all the way from London.'

Reinhold stands and offers his hand, 'Very pleased to meet you, Lyn?'

'You're the saint...according to our Ma Hewett.'

'Ma Hewett?'

Peggy enlightens him, 'She's our resident fortune teller.'

Lyn points across to Ma Hewett's stall at the end of the table and the queue of locals seated, sipping tea and waiting.

'She's obviously very good, but I think she may have me confused with Roger Moore...although I can raise an eyebrow at a push.'

Which Reinhold duly demonstrates. Lyn smiles and probes further, asking,

'So, is this a business trip or pleasure?' Reinhold finishes a mouthful of cake and takes a sip of tea,
'You better ask Ma Hewett that.'

****

A little later, nearing tea-time, the street party stalls begin to pack up as the light fades. Reinhold follows Peggy as she unlocks her front door and enters. Dusty growls and starts chasing her tail in circles. Then something strange happens...she stops, seems transfixed and serene as she shuffle-crawls across, settling by Reinhold's feet. Peggy observes the spectacle in wonderment,
'Have you two been practising that?'
Reinhold laughs, 'I assure you that we've never met before.'
'Well, Hugo, this is Dusty - - '
'Pleased to make your acquaintance Dusty...'
Reinhold bends down and shakes Dusty's paw whilst pretending to whisper to the dog,
'That was better than rehearsals.'
'She prefers 'Trips' to walks these days, courtesy of my brother and his discarded joints,' Peggy informs him with a disgruntled sigh.
'Ah, I see. Well, it sure makes a change from bones.'
'So, take us as you find us. Can I get you a drink? There's Martini,

rum, some scotch, or my brother's got some beer in the fridge.'

'Beer sounds good, if he doesn't mind?'

Peggy hands him a glass from a sideboard.

'Now, you must be hungry?'

Peggy opens the kitchen door, switches on the flourescent light, and comes face-to-face with Sunny, who greets all with a loud snort! Reinhold's evening entertainment just cranked up a notch.

'Well, I couldn't eat a horse if that's what you mean?'

Sunny's whinnies match Peggy's screams as she goes weak-kneed into Reinhold's arms. Dusty goes ape-shit. Davy rushes in, still woozy from the rude awakening, and absorbs the spectacle as Reinhold, cradling his sister, looks up,

'You must be Davy? Quite a party.'

****

As the evening draws on, Peggy sips a Martini, settled next to Reinhold on the sofa. Dusty, relaxed by Reinhold's feet. Davy pours Reinhold a beer, offers him a joint, which Reinhold declines, 'Thanks but I'll be driving back soon and need to stay on the road, let alone the planet.'

Davy shows him Avery's maps...unwraps the Damascus drill bit and the gold filling where it all started. Davy finishes his beer, stands...sways a tad then takes a hit from his joint and from memory, passionately recites a verse from Dylan Thomas as he steers Reinhold's imaginary car and offers some highway code wisdom for their guest,

"Do not go gentle into that good night'...my friend...'cos...'cos... you might have Tarrant's Jag' to contend with.'

Davy fights a tear and slumps back in to his armchair. Reinhold nods and responds,

'Good advice Davy...but hopefully...we'll be home with Tarrant in our tail wind.'

A mildly intoxicated Reinhold smiles, kisses Peggy on the cheek, and gets up from the settee.

As he goes to leave, he remembers something. From his coat pocket, he produces Peggy's Tupperware sandwich container,

'I almost forgot, this is yours.'

Peggy looks confused, as if her returned gift was a metaphor of a severed link.

'No, but I gave you that.' She feels the weight, the weight of a forgotten, stale sandwich?

'And you've left your lunch, here!'

'Did I? D'you think the bread's worth keeping?'

Peggy's mild irritation is kept under wraps as she prises off the Tupperware lid...*prrpp*...and finds a wad of money!

'Ten thousand pounds should cover the next delivery I hope? Similar, raw, unnealed nuggets like before? I have two buyers who'll be in town in the next two to three weeks.'

Davy rises from his armchair and scrutinises the box suspiciously. Reinhold watches him turn the Tupperware box every which way...

'Unless there's a problem Davy?'

'Just looking for the strings man.'

'Oh, I thought the Coal Board was pulling those? I've just handed you a pair of scissors...so to speak.'

Reinhold turns to Peggy, 'Let's hope 'Mother' can keep her secret until then?'

Peggy gives Reinhold a hug and pecks him on the cheek,

'She'll be as good as gold, won't she Davy?'

Davy responds, 'I'll be seeing her soon.' Sunny winnies from the kitchen,

'And a man about a horse.'

ACME

Early next morning, Davy sits on his bed, lights up a joint and massages his aching knee. He looks out the rear window and checks on Sunny, tethered to a washing pole line out the back in their small patio garden. A little later, he emerges from the kitchen and proudly places a washing-up bowl of Rice Krispies on the ground next to Sunny.

Sunny sniffs...can't place the smell? So he sniffs even bigger... tilts his head, trying work out what the faint crackling sound is? It's almost on the tip of his tongue...and now it is! He snuzzles a mouthful and looks over his blinkers,

'What's this?'

'It's Rice Krispies man, my favourite cereal, I've even added some milk...to make them go snap, crackle and pop.'

'*Your* favourite cereal? Well that may well be but my favourite cereal is *oats*...you do know that horses have been eating oats, always had oats and have always needed oats for the most part of their working lives? With a few nice, tasty carrot treats thrown in too.'

'Yeah man, but we're out of oats right now OK? And tasty carrot treats – and you're a pony man, a small little pit pony at that... not a horse.'

Sunny squeals and shakes his head, Davy takes another hit from his spliff and responds,

'OK, it's cool. I'll get you some oats, alright?'

'And carrots, they help you see in the dark you know...gives a *lookout* that edge.'

'OK, OK, I'll pick up some treats too...*after* my shift.'

'You mean...you're leaving me behind? Here...with powder puff, who'll be running rings around me and yapping?'

'It's safer here man...the next dig is too dangerous and you won't fit on the coach.'

'So, suddenly, I'm not too little after all?'

****

At the Pit Head gates, Davy and Deep Harmony crew arrive in a coach with other 'Blacklegs' and an Ostler (Horse Handler) to be greeted by a handful of policeman keeping watch over a restless line of Pickets outside, straddling the closed gated courtyard.

The Eclipse, with bandaged nose, kill-stares Dino through the window and slams his fist against it, but is restrained by two policemen.

Davy exits the coach with the Ostler, as Tarrant watches the activity from inside the colliery main office and steps outside to address Davy through the locked metal barred gates,

'No work today lads, pit's shut.'

'What d'you mean by 'shut' man?'

'It's the opposite of open?'

'That's funny man but these guys need to work, why weren't we told?'

'Because maintenance only found some gas leaks this morning, should be sorted in a couple of days.'

Davy gestures towards the Ostler and says,

'We were gonna check on the stables, weren't sure if the ponies were being fed?'

Tarrant smiles, 'Oh, I checked...they had breakfast in bed as usual, you can take their orders when you see them next. Now be a good hippy lad and hop back on board your magic bus and we'll see you scabs in a couple of days...unless you're a paying customer that is and are planning to pick up the keys before then?'

'You can bank on it man, either me or m' sister Peggy 'll be seeing you soon.'

Davy and the Ostler step back on to the coach. It starts up and slowly pulls away as Pickets jeer and cheer. Davy nods to the other miners seated at the front, who acknowledge the situation as he joins the Deep Harmony crew at the rear and whispers,

'We're going in *tonight*...bring your bathing suits.'

Big Hewett responds, 'Right, see you all at Avery's beach hut.'

****

A dry, crisp night, under a half-moon glow, accompanies Deep Harmony as they approach Avery's fall-out shelter. Big Hewett looks up towards the heavens,

'Wonder what they'll find up there?'

Davy responds philosophically,

'Maybe *the gateway* man, the fourth dimension into the inner realms of our universe...a higher consciousness...it's your chakra man...the third eye.'

Big Hewett rolls his eyes, Taffy responds, 'Like Doctor Spock's three lugholes in Star Trek – the 'Final front-ier'?'

Davy shakes his head, metaphysical discourse is not on the crew's agenda tonight. He unlocks the padlock and gently prises open the metal door...the rusty hinges groan as the crew don helmets and switch on their cap-lamps, ready to take a dip in the old man's indoor swimming pool...

And at that precise moment, Avery's eight year old neighbour's son, Kevin, has a deja-vu moment...it's that creaking noise again, that spooked him last time. Like a door opening...with the same muted voices, but this time no sloshing sound? Gazing beyond his *Dr Who Tardis Airfix model*...and beyond his bedroom curtains, he sees the dark figures and beams of light disappear?! Those aliens are at it again!

'Mam, mam! Mae'r estroniaid hynny yn ôl!' *(Ma! Ma! Those aliens are back!)*

His dad chides his missus for letting the boy watch too much TV, gets up out of his armchair and shouts up the stairs,

Dydw i ddim yn dweud wrthych chi eto, ewch i gysgu!' *(I'm not telling you again, get to sleep!)*

****

Deep Harmony furtively enter Old Man Avery's shed and set foot on dry ground. The crew look relieved, Dino seems baffled by the group euphoria? Big Hewett explains,

'Last time kid, this was a plunge pool.'

The phrase *'Plunge pool'* seems incongruous to Dino, then it all becomes clear and his face drops.

Davy bristles with authority, 'Like I said man, it's a Miocene Caenozoic porous layer and no recent rain, so looks like we have a dry run.' Dino probes further,

'Maybe we may ava to swim a leetle further on in tunnel?'

Davy perceives a frisson of trepidation in the kid's casual remark, 'You *can* swim man, right?'

Big Hewett reassures the kid with a consoling pat on the shoulder,

'Last time, on return, it was only waist high and there's plenty of breathing space in the roof if the worst happens.'

Dino looks cornered and defensive, sneers it off with a bravado shrug. The crew swap concerned glances, Taffy breaks the awkward silence,

'Don't worry boyo, just keep breathing and we'll see your bubbles.'

Deep Harmony embark on the dry tunnel route with Davy's reaffirmed authority leading his crew back through Avery's hand-hewn secret passage. Davy's helmet lamp illuminating the rod-straight forty yard conduit ahead, with its integrated roof air-pockets for water-logged miners.

The mining milieu of the old man's legacy, now as intended from inception, as a gateway and testament to 'Roman' engineering and an homage to their prospecting and wealth.

Avery's living organism, finding new life, the capillary feeding the main artery of seams and tunnels beyond is now reawakened, with its seven percent gradient descent terminating behind an old spent seam A13, its 'blind' sealed-off approach, no doubt named after the WW2 cruiser tank the crew's Face-captain back in 1941 had once operated, a half-mile back from DR40's south side.

The crew's every step passing through a rib cage of roof supports, spruce, oak, and salvaged pit-props. Their every step inured to whatever hardship awaits them, their every step a little

closer to a point in time where nascent events become legends, remembered by some who, many decades from now, may recall that historic tragedy.

THE ASHTRAY

Above them, a lone man on a mission as dark as the soot black night that shrouds him. He fumbles in his pocket for a key to open the padlocked side gate to the Colliery Yard. His every movement encumbered by his old mate, Johnny Walker. Not the latest Radio One DJ, but the spent bottle of Scotch, consumed after seven pints of beer, providing the 'Dutch courage' necessary for Grady to retain *his* 'bottle' for tonight.

Under the dull glow of a yard utility light, he searches in his holdall and finds another key from what could be a jailer's fob chain. He unlocks the Main Office and heads for the Annex Room where, from a top desk drawer, he finds a small steel key to unlock the adjacent metal filing cabinet. As he pulls open the bottom drawer, his wavering torch beam settles on a small, wooden cigar box...he opens it, revealing a tarnished gold-coloured Yale key. A routine that he may have repeated less than a dozen times in that many years, and a routine that repeatedly asked the question – why a cigar box?

He pauses for a moment, and adjusts his foggy focus on the key to that of a haunted glare, as if it's burning an indelible mark in his 'hand of fate', like a cigar being stubbed out by his superior perhaps, in the palm of his hand...Tarrant's ashtray? He lets the key drop and flicks his hand violently, shaking off the imagined searing heat...the scar of conscience.

He leaves the Colliery Office and his timorous thoughts behind, a firm grip of the key now, as the alpha male dominates, propelling him to stride more purposefully across the yard to a corner munitions building...the *POWDER ROOM*. Here, a metal door greets him. It has a black on yellow image of a *SKULL and CROSSBONES* placard. Below which an enamelled red sign, with bold black letters riveted to the door warns:

'EXTREME CAUTION, HIGH EXPLOSIVES, KEEP OUT, NO UNAUTHORISED PERSONNEL BEYOND THIS POINT.'

He inserts the key in the lock...but it doesn't turn? He tries to dismiss a feeling of relief conflicted with the task ahead, but the emotion and any weakness is short-lived...the key tumbler finally clicks and yields, committing him...as the door eases open.

****

Deep Harmony return to the Monastic Cavern, a lower recess level beyond the Dunkirk Retreat 40 seam. For some reason, they all share an instinctive thought to remain quiet...and just listen... Davy addresses the crew,

'Looks like Tarrant's maintenance dudes downed tools...or never got the gig?'

Big Hewett checks the Silver Dart drill and re-attaches Old Man Avery's Damascus 'crusader' and looks up,

'You mean he's got more bull-shit than the Burma Seam?'

'Yeah man...but why? Why even invent the pretence of a leak and a safety check?'

Dino nods his head, working the thought through,

'Because 'ee can a shut up a the mine.'

Taffy asks the crew, 'Yeh kid, you're dead right...but why do that? What will it achieve?'

Davy's knee starts throbbing...he pulls out his wacky-baccy pouch and chews a finger full, a shudder sensation shoots through his shoulders and down his spine as he remembers something Valma said.

'You know man, Valma mentioned a few days ago that she heard Tarrant talking to Grady about the pit-ponies...something about...'If they come up the games up'?'

Taffy analyses that phrase, 'So...he's saying that if the ponies are brought to surface, they'd have to have a good reason?'

Big Hewett offers his theory, 'Or word 'll get out that he'd tried to pull a fast one and sell 'em off?'

Taffy adds another observation, 'Dog food or donkey rides that'll be.'

Now Dino chips in,

'I had-a donkey ride at-a Weston-super-Mare-a, when I was-a twelve...isa the pit-a pony the same-a as-a the donkey?'

Davy's had enough of the crew's captivating ramblings and starts to get frustrated,

'Enough boys! OK?! Who knows man? Maybe it's an RSPCA thing but no way man, we're talking Tarrant – and the mine's on the market and that arsehole's gonna strip every goddamn asset man!'

Taffy chirps in but it's ill-timed, 'You mean assets or asses?'

Davy explodes, 'You think this is funny Taff?! Jeezuz man, let's not waste anymore of our precious time on dog food or...or seaside rides or is a donkey a pit-pony or ass or figuring out how that seedy suit thinks man, because there's one 'asset' he aint never gonna see surface man...' Davy points behind him,

'...and it's right over there dude!'

TO BOLDLY GO

Deep Harmony settle into an efficient working unit, Davy instructing Dino to drill precisely within the strata of rock that is indicated on Avery's map, whilst checking the water hose and sizzling drill bit. Alongside the kid, Big Hewett working and probing with a pick and Taffy shovelling away, checking the debris for any gold fragments. Several hours pass, still no luck. Davy checks the blue lamp flame as the enveloping moist dust clings, coating every square inch of skin and clothing and settling in for the night like weariness itself.

Davy takes another pinch of baccy to ease his chronic knee pain. The atomised rock's stubborn presence seems deliberately suspended, preventing Davy from examining what real progress has been achieved...if any. He waves his arms to create an aperture. But a swirling hollow forms, providing a momentary view in his helmet light of a *'tail'...an amber striation* embedded in the rock, as the agitated, particled fog closes in like a camera lens.

Davy wipes his eyes...and again, as hid vision clouds over. Its as if the *Mother* has deployed some form of masking defence shield, like in Star Trek.

'Boys! Boys! It's there! Look – it was the Dragon's tail man! I saw it, it was right there man!' Davy's inner vision conjures an image beyond the serpent's cloak-shield that follows the tail. A *GIANT GOLDEN CELTIC DRAGON* awakens from its emblematic flag incarnation and breathes FIRE, which transforms in their helmet light beams. Davy vocalises his hallucination,

'It's alive man...it's breathing...can't you feel the heat man?!

The Deep Harmony crew peer through the persistent mist, Big Hewett grabs Davy's shoulder and grabs the wacky-baccy pouch from his hand,

'Look Davy boy, don't do a bloody Pink Floyd on us, not now!'

Davy blinks at the sceptic crew standing shoulder-to-shoulder with Big Hewett...Davy takes a deep breath as the fog clears and nods his head in the direction behind them,

'There's nothing pink about this dragon man...*only gold*...a lot of *gold* man, stretching from its tail to its body...and beyond... What do they say in those pantomimes? *'It's behind you!'*

The non-believers all slowly turn, a mind-set cocktail of caution, doubt and anxiety to validate Davy's theatrical creature...

Dino, Big Hewett, and Taffy stand mesmerised as their cap-lights dance, tracing a glittering *FIVE YARD VEIN OF SPECKLED GOLD*, widening as it disappears into the rock strata, revealing the umbilical to the *MOTHER LODE!*

Dino drops to his knees, awed by the aesthetic, as if praying to Madonna, the Virgin Mary,

'Bellissimo oro!'

Davy looks across and smiles contentedly, as he wipes Old Man Avery's map and carefully refolds it, placing it back in a protective plastic bag, as he quotes,

'This is the voyage of...Deep Harmony man! To explore strange new worlds, to seek out new life...to boldly go where no man has gone before.'

****

At the Pit-Head, Grady checks his holdall for the second time, the visual realisation of the task weighs heavy, as if it's joined to his hip. He steps into the cage, pulls the grill across, which clanks and echoes in the shaft...almost fade-blending into another feint noise...like somebody drilling? For a still second he dwells on that...then pushes the thought aside and pushes the lever forward...the cage starts to descend...

THE FAN

A pool of rippling *GOLDEN WATER* settles as the crew stop a merry triumphal dance and resume excavation. Davy helps Dino with precise drilling, as GOLD nodules fizz past them and fall away into the water hose spray like golden hail-stones. Obsessive activity, bordering on hysteria, as Deep Harmony drill, dig and bag, in a sweat-bath of bare torsos. Big Hewett's pick extracts an endless vein of GOLD NUGGETS, which Taffy scrambles in the water to retrieve and deposit in a coal sack...

Nobody notices the safety lamp flame pulse, putter, and slyly lower.

A distant *MASSIVE TREMOR* makes Davy stop Dino drilling as cascades of water dislodge the drill-bit. A mile back towards the Pit-Head, Grady's sabotage assignment resonates...

The crew stop everything, stand dead still, unable to hear anything beyond the intimidating hiss of gushing water... something isn't right...Davy shouts to Dino,

'Kill the water man!' Dino struggles with the supply hose's twist-tap...the deluge of water pressure builds...

'Come on kid, turn it clockwise!' Dino panics, fights with the control, but no dice,

'I am Meester Johnson! I am! The hose-a is-a turned off!'

Big Hewett slosh-strides over and grabs the drill and hose,

'Give it here boy.' Big Hewett wrestles with the tube attachment, assisted by Davy...both study the geyser of water spray around the drill-bit...Taffy quips, masking his fear,

'I think Mother's water's have broken!'

Big Hewett's hand goes numb, Davy takes over... Now the pressure's like a fire-hose! Davy curses aloud,

'Shit! Shit! It's no good man!'

He checks it with his gloved hand, only this time it's a torrent of pressure attacking the back of his hand? What in hell is going on?! On the rock-face, cobweb fractures spread like a virus on the scissored *Dragon's tail*. Hairlines strafe at speed...if rock ever thawed in some imagined subterranea it would make this sound. A loud burbling rumble follows...

Davy pulls out the old man's map, now the hippy's desperate sixth sense operating. He scours the detail, finger tracing synaptic strands and labels...as he subconsciously taps his 'third eye' for insight,

'To Fan? *Fan?* To the...bloody *Fan*?!'

Suddenly his body floods with realisation,

'Oh my God. Shit man – everybody out! Now! It's a spring!'

Big Hewett shouts above the relentless down-rush of water, as Taffy and Dino's eyes fix on rising amber water, level edging above their thighs,

'Spring? What spring?!'

'The Fan! It's not a vent man – it's a river! *The River Fan*!'

WH-O-O-O-SH! Without warning, a hydrant of water tears through the seam like an aqua-jet, bulldozes the crew to the back of the cavern in a swirling tide, as two pit props give way on a side wall of rock, collapsing by the Cavern entrance and sealing their exit...

HIS NIBS

Next day, late afternoon, outside the Colliery Office, Valma meets Peggy,

'I told him you were coming.'

'Thanks Pet.'

Valma leads Peggy through to Tarrant's office, she knocks on the door and pops her head in,

'Davy Johnson's sister's here, she's got something for you.'

Peggy enters wearing a red PVC jacket and matching mini-skirt with her all-business smile as Tarrant gestures for her to take a seat. Peggy plonks down a small stack of Tupperware containers and the *contract* on Tarrant's desk next to a flower vase, knocking over his model winch-wheel in the process and scattering his neat row of pens – the lady means business. Valma steadies the flower vase from becoming a further casualty and fights back a smile as Tarrant fusses over restoring desk order and looks up peevishly,

'Sure you don't want catering luv'?'

Peggy touches her dangling gold earring, real casual like, crosses her legs slowly, almost playfully, and fixes Tarrant in her heavy mascara gaze,

'It's all there, what you discussed with my brother, Davy...twenty grand.'

Tarrant leans forward and picks up one of the pink Tupperware tubs,

'Twenty K eh? Does that come with every set?'

'No luv'. Offer ends today. You see, there's a tea-room up for sale too...my brother's never tried catering.'

Tarrant grabs the contract...thumbs through it...he's impressed, but tries to hide it as his eyes flick suspiciously to Valma.

'You're *finished* love – I can deal with this.' Valma hears the implied threat but responds with new found courage,

'Think I best stay Mr Tarrant, as you'll need a witness...won't you?'

Tarrant's stern jaw tightens, he removes the lids. *'Pphht...pphht...'* On the table he extracts the contents...a pile of banknotes build. He looks at the map he marked for Grady, lying open on the floor and keeps the smile for later,

'You do realise, there's no Co-op dividend stamps with this?'

Peggy feigns disappointment,

'Really? Oh well...that new kettle will just 'ave to wait.'

Tarrant adds, 'And...no...*refund* once it's signed?'

Peggy hands Tarrant a plastic Biro pen which seems to hover over his Mont Blanc and Parker pens below...almost like they were looking up in disgust. He clicks it several times and tries to sign the contract, but the ballpoint's dry. He writes Peggy off with a look, bins the ballpoint, and under his breath comments, 'Cheap.' He takes a Sheaffer fountain pen from his inside pocket, slowly unscrews the top and *signs the two contract copies*. Peggy's next...she goes to take Tarrant's fountain pen, but he hands her a Parker ballpoint from the desk and delves out some etiquette tips,

'One shouldn't use another man's fountain pen sweetheart...it's just not done, nibs get used to their owners and their style.'

Peggy responds as she signs, 'Now m' brother would say that... *stiles and pens* sounds like a lot of horse-shit.' Valma can't control a snigger as she witnesses their signatures and signs.

Flirtatiously, Tarrant teases Peggy with her signed copy, holding it just out of reach as he looks down her cleavage, and beyond to her white ankle boots, standing next to the map,

'Careful...it's wet.'

Peggy stands up and with a firm grip, snatches it away. Tarrant loses his hold and pulls back, knocking Valma's flower vase over onto the desk. Flowers and water spill onto the map, spattering his leaking pen and crotch. Peggy looks down at the dripping, ink-stained patch between his trouser legs and looks at Valma, 'He's right luv', his nib is leaking...must be the excitement.'

Tarrant's dour expression follows Peggy and Valma to the door as they exit. He grinds his molars and from a lower desk drawer produces a bottle of cognac and a glass tumbler. He pours himself a celebratory shot as he opens a tin of cigarillos and lights one. He returns the individual stacks of money to the Tupperware containers and reseals the lids, *pphht, pphht...*

almost gets a kick from the novelty of it all – serious wads of cash in plastic tubs.

He gazes at the signed contract, and at the flowers, scattered wreath-like on the map. He raises his glass,

'Here's to a miner's wet dream...R.I.P.'

'Susurrador de Caballos'

So, I expect you're wondering what happened to Deep Harmony that night?

Well, legend has it that they all retired to Spain...so they must have survived? Right? Or, more likely, it might have been Italy for that matter, 'cos of the Dino connection thing. Legends do that don't they? They have that malleable bespoke characteristic going on, embellished to suit the pub narrator?

Now, a village local who had worked at the colliery as a young lad, and has since long retired, said he'd heard a rumour about a large villa in Spain, owned by a miner. It was called 'Acme', but locals preferred it's Spanish translation, 'La Cumbre'. Understandable really, as 'Acme' is not the most fetching name for a Mediterranean beach house with an azure-blue, vista-view of the ocean In fact, it almost sounds like a skin complaint, which is why one remembers it, I suppose...and now, come to think of it...wasn't that the name of a whistle?

Then there was George's Barber Shop on the High Street in Merthyr Tydfil – where someone who worked at the Gent's hairdressers said he'd heard a story from a client about another coastal property his boss had rented in Spain, called 'Rincon Soleado' ...Spanish for 'Sunny Corner'. Now, the chap who owned it, he described as a bit 'alternative', shall we say...he had a limp and a pigtail, wore sandals and kept ponies. He was known by the locals as the 'Susurrador de Caballos' the 'Horse Whisperer'. He said it was quite a posh place and he reckoned the owner looked like some drug baron, with that limp...like he'd been shot or something. Which would account for the swanky 'Ponderosa' spread, as he put it...and this black guy, his right arm man, who literally had just that, a right arm and...get this...his neighbour, who he never spoke to, only saw him from a distance once, definitely wasn't Spanish but was all dressed-up like some Matador. He was the bloke who owned 'La Cumbre'.

He said this place in Alicante was being developed by some London outfit, Reingold Construction or something...not far from where they had a guided tour around some ancient mines in Leon – 'Las Medulas' I think he said...s'posed to be the largest gold pit dating back to the Roman Empire, hidden under the Eria Valley – it wasn't worth the visit he said, as you didn't see much... it's all vegetable crops now. He also said he went back again, a few years later 'cos his wife is Spanish and has relatives there, anyway, she'd heard that the local planning authority had objected to them wanting to build some massive stable right on the border of this heritage valley site at the back of Sunny Corner. They'd already allowed them to build another villa called 'Lulu' with an aviary and, also in the province, a trattoria come tapas bar run by a young chap...snappy dresser, neat short hair, who was often getting into fights with rowdy Brit' tourists.

You know, a person could speculate on all these stories and so-called 'events' past, for a lifetime...and more often than not, people do just that, don't they?

So, let me save you the trouble...and...as far as I know, tell you what really happened after 'Mother's waters' broke in the early hours that morning...

"Look after the senses and the sounds will look after themselves"
Lewis Carroll, Alice in Wonderland

The aftermath from Grady's initial detonation needed no follow up, as planned. In fact, it was more than he or Tarrant had bargained on. In the Cavern, Deep Harmony's drilling had released a lethal cocktail of methane and CO gases, billowing downwind as the dynamite explosion dislodged the central ventometer, causing friction as the fan-blade tips catch – chag-chag-chag – and jam.

Now...the hot metal fan-casing begins to glow and spark, the cavern's emanating dust particles ignite in the shaft – VROOMMTH! A BLINDING FLASH, cannons, a resonant air current back down the mine's roadway towards DR40, where...

The crew slam against the cave siding like spat-out discharge from an effluent pipe. Then, as if trapped in some cavernous rinse cycle, are tumble-swept further back into an unknown passage, extending beyond the Monastic seam. Taffy fights to keep his gold-laden holdall and Dino afloat, as they flounder in the rising flood-water,

'We all gonna die?! Please Meester Johnson! No!' Big Hewett manages to stand momentarily, his weary hulk pummelled but head firm and steady...long enough for his helmet light to see they are trapped in a water-filled, dark chamber with the pressure pinning them to the rock face.

Davy manages to clamber out with his treasure holdall, onto a high ledge, an out-crop that his light-beam scans beyond...into a tunnel...only to find darkness...

Big Hewett pats his swag bag with an ironic smile and shouts above the rushing water and Dino's panic cries,

'Davy boy! 'To have and have not' as they say eh Captain?!' Big Hewett's mawkish proclamation seems to dissolve in the dark waters and the crew's darker thoughts of accepting their fate...

But beyond the corporeal, Davy's visceral consciousness becomes aware of a distant, yet distinct, high-pitched sound... something he has heard before...drug-induced maybe...that time in hospital perhaps? He listens hard...tuning out from the ramblings and surrendering sighs of his crew,

'*Quiet!* Can't you hear that man?! It's coming from this tunnel man! Can't you *'feel'* it brothers?!'

Davy thumps his heart and prods his forehead with firm conviction.

Big Hewett shakes his head in disbelief, he's tired to the marrow and could rest now for a long, long spell...

'That third eye of yours playing up again brother Davy...in that pot-head of yours?'

Davy gets to his knees, winces with the pain, fishes out his sodden wacky-baccy pouch and chews as he turns to face the dark hole ahead...the piercing sound is now unquestionable,

'It's that whistle man! Like Old Man Avery's...come on boys, follow me...we're being rescued!'

The crew stare into the black hole that will soon fill with water, Taffy calls out,

'That could be even worse...that wasn't on the map was it?! And...what whistle?!'

Big Hewett responds,

'Davy...for Christ-sakes nobody can hear it...nobody, only you boyo...only you!'

Davy turns back to them as the whistle becomes even more persistent,

'You can't hear that?!'

Dino, breathing heavily over chin-lapping water, splutters a respectful reply,

'I *believe* you Meester Johnson...we all gotta follow our Captain... we not-a gonna die in thees-a monastery horror-a chamber!'

Dino's endorsement reboots Davy's morale,

'So, you hear it too man?'

Dino stays uncomfortably silent but pulls away and splash-flounders towards his Captain, so Taffy has to hold on, to keep him afloat. Big Hewett tags on then, power-strides through the tide, pushing to the front to pull man and boy to the ledge.

Davy hauls Dino up as Big Hewett shoves Taffy and his bullion-bag onto the outcrop. Dino helps Davy pull Big Hewett up...they all collapse on the ledge, inches above the rising water level. Only Davy's helmet lamp is now functioning and all eyes fix on the single weak beam, swallowed by the black oblivion ahead...

****

Late that afternoon on the day Peggy and Valma left Tarrant's office, they walked out of the Colliery Yard side gate and got into Peggy's red mini. Where a jubilant Peggy kissed the contract, leaving a pink lipstick imprint just below the witness signature,

'Oops...could almost be a sort of Royal seal.'

And through that same side gate, earlier that morning, Grady had returned to report his 'mission accomplished', so-to-speak.

In Tarrant's office, Grady tosses the Powder Room key onto his desk...it clinks against the model black winch-wheel and leaves a bright chink. He sits himself down, without asking, like he did before, and gives Tarrant the breaking news,

'So much for your R and D techies...seems your boffins missed the little detail of...a bleedin' river running through it!'

'What?! What are you saying?!'

'I'm saying that the first blast opened the bloody flood gates Tarrant – that mine may as well be a wishing well now.'

Tarrant takes it in, his thin lips forming something between a smile and a smirk, that seems to disgust Grady, who gets up to leave,

'So...we're done here?'

'Yes mate...rather...'Well' I'd say.'

'And your hippy's gonna drop some coins into the fountain and then maintenance will make the unfortunate discovery? What, tomorrow? Before it *leaks out*...so to speak?'

'Something like that.'

Grady's contempt is tangible, 'How d'you sleep at night Tarrant?'

Tarrant looks out of the window...across the valleys...

'Easy here isn't it? You can count the sheep...I'm going to miss that.'

****

Earlier that same morning, Lucky, the black Labrador, had returned and could be heard barking in the back garden, which Mrs Avery went to investigate. Tottering carefully out of her kitchen with her limited vision, she could just make out the faint silhouettes of a string of pit-ponies that had mysteriously gathered and were enjoying the tasty carrot patch near the Fallout shelter.

This spectacle was under close scrutiny by her neighbour's son, Kevin, who informed Mrs Avery over the fence on his way to school about what had happened.

As he enlightens Mrs Avery in infinite detail about the cosmos, Noah's Ark, and other *other-worldly* matters, he points to the evidence...the equine visitors,

'That's...'*Floyd'*, *'Emily'*, *'Spike'* and...uh...'*Rocket!'* – it says so on their harnesses...the aliens returned and brought them up, I saw them.'

Mrs Avery manages a frail nod, 'Really? I see...' as she turns around and goes back inside, followed by Lucky, who looks back at the boy with, what one might perceive as a, *'Yeah, right'*, dismissive look.

****

Not long after Peggy's little red mini leaves the scene, Tarrant steps out of his office, locks up and strolls across to his very big Jag', where he pops the car boot, slings the Tupperware money boxes inside, and slams it shut. He slap-pats his hands as if wiping away the detritus of cheap, pink plastic, then notices the dark ink stain on his suit crotch, like a Rorschach test blot of his true character, initiated by Peggy the 'shrink'.

By the colliery gates, a straggle-bag of Union Pickets with the Eclipse (sporting a nose-plaster) and two Police Officers, have returned and stand with strike placards, ready to intervene with any blackleg coach arrivals. Tarrant calls out to the Eclipse,

'Didn't your brother tell you about the gas leak?'

The Eclipse's face: a mask of uninformed anger,

'What leak?! Nuh, I 'aven't seen 'im.'

Tarrant informs the bunch,

'No? Well, there's health and safety checks going on, so...I'd give it a couple of days lads.'

He lets them dwell on that for a nano-beat, then with a casual firmness says,

'Open the gates if you would?'

He checks a blemish on the Jag's gleaming paintwork before getting in. He turns the ignition key as the radio blasts out *The Beatles, 'Revolution'.*

As his back wheels reverse, a discrete *FAULT LINE CRACK* zig-zags from behind the office and heads for the colliery gates! Pickets, Police, and the Eclipse feel the ground slightly *SHIFT* beneath them. One of the huge metal gates *TILTS, just a little... and jams*. The Police Officers help the Eclipse try to open the gate for Tarrant, who is oblivious to the geological activity resulting from his game-plan with the Eclipse's brother.

Tarrant impatiently blows his horn and winds down the window, shouting over the blaring car radio,

'Today if possible matey!'...but the gates aren't budging. He gets out and walks across to the Policemen and the Eclipse, wrestling with the metal gates,

'Do I have to do everything 'round here?!'

He grabs hold of the gate, assumes a straddle-stance and...with a monstrous effort, heaves as the *FAULT LINE,* like a voltage zap, passes under the Jag', between Tarrant's legs! The *GATES COLLAPSE* and fall away as the back-wheels of Tarrant's Jag' *CRUNK DOWNWARDS* into the earth, causing the boot to fly open before *DISAPPEARING BACKWARDS INTO A YAWNING CHASM!*

All heads turn, open-mouthed, watching Gaia swallow the Jag' whole, accompanied by the fading soundtrack of *The Beatles' 'Revolution'.* The sealed Tupperware containers 'break-out' as if making their escape, and tumble down into the distant gold-tinged receding flood-water, floating away like a pink flotilla...

****

Many weeks later, in the Cambrian Mountains of Snowdonia, on a windswept barren landscape, Davy and Valma approach Adam and Eve, *two isolated columns of rock known to Welsh speaking locals as 'Sion a Siân',* just as he remembered from Old Man Avery's photo where time seemed to stand still in Tryfan.

Valma looks up at the granite monoliths, resolutely planted a fair stretch apart,

'Davy...are you sure you want to do this...with that knee of yours?'

Davy's eyes dart from one obelisk to the other...a good yard and a bit apart with a sheer drop onto unforgiving rock...*what are the chances with that gammy leg of his?* He massages his knee and lights up a joint,

'Eternal happiness man, according to the legend...Old Man Avery made the leap...years ago...it's cool.'

He sits, takes another hit from the joint and lies back...listening to a cuckoo call...

'Valma, d'you hear that?'

Valma listens, strains to attune to Davy's mind-scape,

'What Davy?'

'The bird song man...that's a cuckoo.' He points to the East, squeezes Valma's hand and smiles as he lies back onto a grassy verge, letting his mind meld into the landscape...

THE REMAINING TWO PIT-PONIES, 'Robbie' and 'Sultan' never made the climb back through Old Man Avery's secret tunnel... sure, just like Davy did, they heard that spirit-whistle, animals have that sixth sense operating don't they? And those big ears. But making their escape to higher ground was more than a stretch at their time of life...

...some are luckier than others in that respect.

And just like Davy, Sunny's escape was a dream come true. Back at number 79, Pitman's Row, Peggy and Davy looked at a stack of pink Tupperware containers on the coffee table, found floating down the mine...

'Looks like we got our refund after all.'

...as they watched 'The Magnificent Seven' on TV, with Sunny stood behind the settee, peering over his blinkers, and their shoulders, at that classic 'Riding Shotgun' scene with Yul Brynner in that 'don't-mess-with-me' black outfit as he lights the coolest mini cigarillo ever, boosting Hamlet cigar sales for decades. Meanwhile, the so-cool-you-could-skate-on-him, Steve McQueen, checks the breech of his shot-gun and...wait for it...test shakes those cartridges like maracas. Sunny's all eyes on the HORSE hitched to the wagon as Davy takes a hit from his joint and notices what he, strangely, never really noticed before...it's Sunny...who smiles and winks at him...

And as 'luck' would have it...Peggy never did win the Tupperware Gold Agent prize – that trip to Spain...but later that year, Reinhold surprised her and took her on a 'POSH' cruise, to the real Spain, a place in Alicante, unspoilt and undeveloped, near Leon...

AFTER THE FLOODING, Davy confided in Deep Harmony that he'd had a recurring dream...

'More of a nightmare man.'

...considering that one minute Pennant's head was there and then the next minute, somehow, either before or during the flood, it got mislaid... In his dream-state, he saw a gold-encrusted skull, almost Buddha-like, watching over them...

'So, that's a sign man, right? That he's with us now...with the gold, and cool with us being scabs? Right boys?'

Deep Harmony chew that one over, as he also assured them in whispered tones, over many pints of beer in their local Griffin pub, that it was a 'Miocene Caenozoic porous layer man'...

...to which the crew, in deep harmonious tones, replied in a choir-like chorus,

'So it'll drain!'

AT THE VILLAGE ORACLE'S household, in that small stone terraced cottage opposite Taffy and Lyn's, Ma Hewett drops some fish food flakes into the goldfish bowl sitting on her window sill... as she looks out, she sees a delivery van from Peggy's furniture store, Hardy's, delivering Lyn's new sideboard. The fish seem to be watching too...coal and gold together, suspended in water, in broad daylight...who'd have twigged that...ever?

SO... *'THUS GREW THE TALE OF WONDERLAND':*

'Slowly, one by one, its quaint events were hammered out and now the tale is done, and home we steer, a merry crew, beneath the setting sun. Alice! A childish story take, and, with a gentle hand, lay it where childhood's dreams are twined In memory's mystic band, like pilgrim's wither'd wreath of flowers pluck'd in a far-off land.'

Lewis Carroll, Alice in Wonderland: The Complete Collection

Glossary terms

⚙ *'Quite frankly my dear'- is a line from the 1939 film 'Gone with the Wind' starring Clark Gable and Vivien Leigh. The line is spoken by the Hollywood screen idol Rhett Butler, as his last words to Scarlett O'Hara in response to her tearful question: "Where shall I go? What shall I do?"*

⚙ *'Ventometer': large fan deployed in mine shafts to extract carbon monoxide and other poisonous gases.*

⚙ *Cutty Sark: was a clipper ship built in Dumbarton in 1869 and was one of the fastest vessels of its day. It is also an archaic Scottish name for a short nightdress.*

⚙ *Cuddly trifle: phrase to describe the physicality of a colourful wobbly object.*

⚙ *Beads and lentils: refers to typical adornments associated with 'Hippy chicks/females'*

⚙ *Chit: a piece of paper.*

⚙ *A 'Gas': Hippy vernacular/term used in the Sixties to describe something euphoric.*

⚙ *The mining terms such as 'G30': due to the labyrinth and volume of mining tunnels codes using letters and numbers were required.*

⚙ *NUM: the National Union of Mineworkers is a trade union for coal miners in Great Britain, formed in 1945 from the Miners' Federation of Great Britain.*

⚙ *Stent: The coalface would be divided into sections (stents) of about 8 to 10 yards in length, e.g. a coalface 150 yards long would have 15 to 18 stents. A collier/miner would work his stent supporting the roof as the coal was removed.*

⚙ *Beat: A screenwriting term meaning 'a pause'.*

⚙ *Hawser: a chain or steel cable used to haul heavy loads.*

THE WELSH DRAGON HAS WINGS…
Davy and his crew's journey continues in Spain
courtesy of Freddy Laker's ground-breaking
trans-continental budget flights in the forthcoming
novel 'Viva Deep Harmony'…

Speaking of 'ground breaking' on foreign shores…
here's a little teaser…

ward, do I make myself clear?!'

She about turns and leaves the gathering in what one would best describe as a military march.

Davy looks at his visitors somewhat perplexed.

'What's eating her man?'

Peggy's first to respond and uses a leaflet she is holding like a baton to emphasise her point,

'That Davy, is *definitely* a line of enquiry I would not pursue.'

Taffy and Big Hewett nod in agreement... Dino is still checking the Sister out further down the ward and is in two minds...

Davy's eyes can't stop following the Mediterranean blue on Peggy's leaflet as it seems to flaunt its continental colour against the drab grey hospital décor, with the flair of a Flamenco dancer.

'What's with the leaflet Sis'?'

Peggy unfolds the brochure, *'Viva Espana! Welcome to Sunny Spain!'* As she explains,

'It's a holiday brochure... Hugo and I were thinking of flying to Alicante'

"Hugo and I' now is it?' Davy squints as he misreads the bright yellow heading,

'Spain?! *Welcome Sunny to... Spain...* Sis', we'd never get him on the plane.'

'Hugo's flown before, don't think there's a problem there?'

'Not Hugo, *Sunny*...it says it on the brochure...it's a sign man, the Arch Duke is at it again.'

Big Hewett sits forward,

'Davy, there's no way they'd let a pit pony fly budget class.'

'Way up? Way up where man?' Davy readjusts himself as if the answer requires repositioning...his eyeline following his high flung leg to the ceiling and beyond...

The Sister Nurse enlightens him,

'Heaven. First time it was rocks falling on you down there, then you up here falling on them, what you planning next...dropping from the sky?'

Davy responds, 'Everything happens for a reason man...'

Davy's gaze is still fixed on the beyond... beyond his plaster-cast foot as he informs her that...

'The Dude Architect had it all planned from cot to colliery man...when me mum pushed my pram back and forth every day through the door of opportunity...an atomic 79 man and we never heard the explosion man...all those years ago through time man...until now... here... in '69... the Arch' Dude must've have been smiling'.

The Sister Nurse shakes her efficient head at the hallucinatory ramblings and checks Davy's chart...particularly the medication prescribed bit...

'I think we can reduce the morphine dosage tonight'.

Davy tugs the Sister's uniform sleeve...something unintentionally intimate in that moment but that's how it looks, as he hesitates, looking for a thumbs up from his visitors to impart the big secret... before bending forward and earnestly asking in confidence,

'Do you know what '69 *really* means to me...and you...and all of us?'

The Sister Nurse extracts her sleeve from his grasp and straightens herself, scours at the prurient group around the bed,

'Mr Johnson we will not tolerate salacious behaviour on this

'Look Valma it's cool, ok? I wouldn't do it if I didn't think...I *could* do it?'

Davy's proclamation ends up sounding more like a question.

'Davy, what *you* think, may not relate to what *this* stone slab has got planned'.

She slap-pats it again, the chilling solid thud of flesh hitting stone...a sound effect that resonates with Davy's fate...

'Eternal happiness man...' Davy's words seem to hang there... suspended, like his committed leap between the sisters of rock as he launches himself...

****

Early evening at the local District Post War Memorial Hospital, Davy, with leg plaster in a sling complemented by a matching head-plaster sits upright in, what possibly may be the same ward bed from his last encounter with Mother Earth's rocks. His sister Peggy, Big Hewett, Taffy and Dino are gathered around, as a shapely mature Sister Nurse adjusts the leg-sling tension to an angle resembling a salute. Davy winces as she dryly asks, 'I hear you're working your way up in the world?'

Davy looks confused and bleary-eyed from the pain killers and asks,

VIVA DEEP HARMONY

On that windswept barren landscape of Snowdonia, perched on 'Sion', a column of rock in the Cambrian Mountains, Davy Johnson looks across the void to its stone-cold granite sister 'Sian' and swallows hard as he takes a hit from his wacky-baccy spliff.

Below this edifice, Valma looks up and shakes her head at the poised hippy circus act,

'Davy, you don't have to do this, y'know that don't you? When *Old* Man Avery made that leap all those years ago, he was a *young* man Avery... y' don't have to prove anything to me?'

Davy gingerly adjusts his footing and takes a deep breath as Valma pats the rock like a giant gravestone, with a plea to go easy on him as she prays,

'Please Sion, tell your sister...not to be so hard on that crazy miner up there who's about to jump her!'

FANCY BEING A GOLD PROSPECTOR?

'This is far out man, you dig?!'
Deep Harmony's quest may be over for now but yours may have just begun...
Somewhere in Wales, as marked on the treasure map herein...four coins forged from pure Gold, each embossed with an intricate gold skull relief facia, lie buried...
Yes, you heard that right first time, where Aur Cymru the rarest gold in the world can be found, in the form of mesmerising unique skull jewellery, FOUR GOLD COINS are waiting to be discovered, each worth £5000 – the only four ever minted in the world!
In the four corners of Wales, amidst a legacy of coal mines that once were, a hidden collective coin treasure named after the Deep Harmony crew still remains...and could be yours to treasure...
Davy, Taffy, Big Hewett and Dino.
Numerous clues are already hidden in the text of this novel linked to riddles, prose, cyphers and codes found in <u>CLUELESS</u> products...including tea, coffee, canned drinks, short stories and clothing.
Who said 'There's no gold where there's coal?'...

GOOD LUCK PROSPECTORS!!

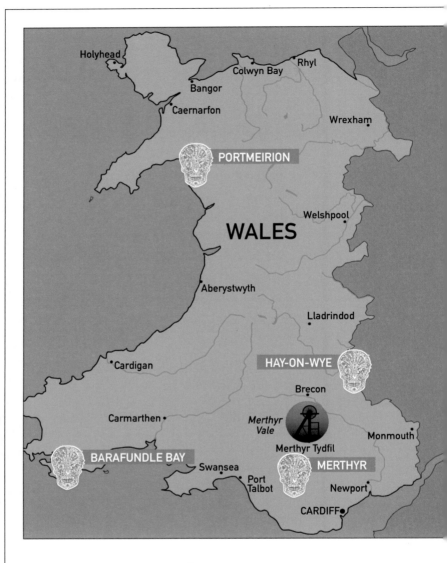

Merthyr
Vale

Buried Welsh gold skull
embossed coin locations

'Taffy gestures Peggy to have a peek at the leaflet adding,
'He's right Davy...plus...why Alicante Peg'? What's so special about this place?'
Dino surprises the group, 'Eet isa bella region, Leon ees in the Eria Valley...very romantic...the Romans were beeg there...as an empire...I theenk they mined there.'
Big Hewett adds, 'Doesn't sound like much of a holiday Peg', more a sort of 'Coals to Newcastle' break I'd say'.
Peggy smiles...a smile that holds a secret,
'Who said anything about coal?'

A NOVEL IDEA THAT COULD CHANGE YOUR LIFE

BOOKS *Books* BOOKS books BOOKS

A book can change a life and we love them all from ABC Children's to XYZ Spiritual. we love creative people. geniuses and we cherish authors.

If you have written any kind of book be it pure text or illustrated or a combination of the two, we want to get your book printed, distributed, sold and read by everyone.

It does not matter if it is a book on Spirituality, Religion, Romance, a Children's Story, a Biography, Your Memoirs, Business, Money, Entrepreneurialism, Inspirational, Self Help, a Cookbook, Food, Photography, Science Fiction, a Manual or even your Project.

We can print one book or a million plus books. Imagine seeing your book in print, sharing your creative genius, thoughts and passion with anyone and everyone? You love it, we will love it, and we will get your book out there through our one-stop-shop of self-publishing.

CLUELESS COULD BE THE CUSTODIAN OF YOUR CREATIVITY

The 'literal' and embedded traditional route of 'Gatekeepers' and incompetent publishers is an arduous and costly process and often literary treasures get rejected due to publisher's trends and marketing requirements. Often decisions can coincide with a 'Gatekeeper' reader's bad day or bad 5 minutes! Even J K Rowling after a dozen rejections from publishers was told, *'You will never make money out of Harry Potter'*...

With CLUELESS the audience decides, so, if it's good, let us get it out there through book wholesalers, retailers, book fairs and via the internet in options of printed, digital and audio formats.

TYPESETTING

We will professionally typeset your book with the right formatting and in fonts and sizes that you choose. We know only too well that a book's layout is a crucial component of the reader's overall experience.

GRAPHIC DESIGN

'Never judge a book by its cover?' Well, subliminally we all do! So, we're passionate about creative graphic design that helps showcase your writing to sell and tell the story of what is behind the cover. Our graphic designers will committedly work with you to produce the specific eye-catching layout wrapping that captures the essence of your book and the story that lies within...